**'It's very q
though, yo
peaceful.'**

'Meaning you think I'm a city girl and I'm only down here for a short spell?' Jassie looked at him quizzically. 'You really don't have any faith in me at all, do you?'

'If you want my honest opinion…no, I don't,' Alex replied. 'I don't think you'll be able to handle this job. No matter what you say to the contrary.'

'I'm not going to be able to convince you simply by telling you that I can cope, am I? The only way I'll be able to do that is to show you.'

When **Joanna Neil** discovered Mills & Boon®, her lifelong addiction to reading crystallised into an exciting new career writing Medical Romance™. Her characters are probably the outcome of her varied lifestyle, which includes working as a clerk, typist, nurse and infant teacher. She enjoys dressmaking and cooking at her Leicestershire home. Her family includes a husband, son and daughter, an exuberant yellow Labrador and two slightly crazed cockatiels.

Recent titles by the same author:

PRACTISING PARTNERS
THE CHILDREN'S DOCTOR

THE CITY-GIRL DOCTOR

BY

JOANNA NEIL

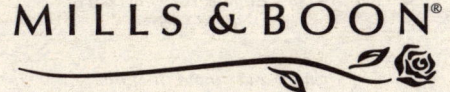

DID YOU PURCHASE THIS BOOK WITHOUT A COVER?

If you did, you should be aware it is **stolen property** as it was reported *unsold and destroyed* by a retailer. Neither the author nor the publisher has received any payment for this book.

All the characters in this book have no existence outside the imagination of the author, and have no relation whatsoever to anyone bearing the same name or names. They are not even distantly inspired by any individual known or unknown to the author, and all the incidents are pure invention.

All Rights Reserved including the right of reproduction in whole or in part in any form. This edition is published by arrangement with Harlequin Enterprises II B.V. The text of this publication or any part thereof may not be reproduced or transmitted in any form or by any means, electronic or mechanical, including photocopying, recording, storage in an information retrieval system, or otherwise, without the written permission of the publisher.

This book is sold subject to the condition that it shall not, by way of trade or otherwise, be lent, resold, hired out or otherwise circulated without the prior consent of the publisher in any form of binding or cover other than that in which it is published and without a similar condition including this condition being imposed on the subsequent purchaser.

MILLS & BOON and MILLS & BOON with the Rose Device are registered trademarks of the publisher.

*First published in Great Britain 2002
Harlequin Mills & Boon Limited,
Eton House, 18-24 Paradise Road, Richmond, Surrey TW9 1SR*

© Joanna Neil 2002

ISBN 0 263 83057 8

*Set in Times Roman 10½ on 12½ pt.
03-0302-47386*

*Printed and bound in Spain
by Litografia Rosés, S.A., Barcelona*

CHAPTER ONE

JASSIE looked across the cobbled forecourt to where the welcoming lights of the Harbour Inn glinted invitingly, and felt a warm glow start up inside her. That was just what she needed, after the long journey she'd had...somewhere bright and cheerful where she could stay for the night, and the prospect of a hot meal.

Glancing around, she saw a group of people making their way towards the entrance of the inn, hurrying to avoid the rain. Another lightning bolt jaggedly speared the grey skyline, and she pulled her jacket around herself more closely, hurriedly turning back to the car and pulling open the boot. Taking out her medical bag, she tried to do the same with her overnight bag, but it snagged on something and stubbornly refused to budge.

'Uh-oh.' Frowning, Jassie peered into the darkened boot, and tried tugging at the holdall while rain splattered the tawny mass of her hair and wreaked havoc with the wealth of natural curls that spilled onto her shoulders. Pushing the damp tendrils away from her eyes, she made a rueful face. Her hair was wild and unruly at the best of times, and it would be even more difficult to tame after this downpour.

'Do you need any help with that?' The male voice was deep and steady, and Jassie paused in her efforts, glancing up as a man came to stand by her side. He looked to be in his mid-thirties, and he was easily a head taller than she was, around six feet. In the fading light she saw that his face was strong boned, the jaw firmly angled, his eyes a compelling dark gold, frank and calmly assessing. His hair was jet black, crisply cut and glistening with droplets of rain. 'I can see you're struggling, and it's not the best of nights to be held up.'

'Thanks, but I think I can manage,' she murmured. 'The strap must be caught on something, that's all. I keep bits and pieces for the car in here...a foot pump and a tyre wrench. It seems to be tangled up in that lot.'

She pulled at the strap for a moment or two longer, conscious that he hadn't moved away but was watching her efforts with interest. 'My fingers are cold,' she explained. 'That's why it's taking me longer than it ought. The car's heater has never been very efficient and it finally gave up on me altogether several miles back.' There had been nothing to combat the rawness of a late spring day and now she was chilled to the bone.

'Let me try,' he said, peering into the boot. He gave his attention to the strap for a moment or two, and then murmured, 'I think I can see where the problem is.'

He freed it in a matter of seconds, and she winced. She was usually very capable and efficient...as a GP she was used to handling all sorts of difficult situations, and it annoyed her that she should need someone else to help her with a simple bag.

'There you are. It was caught up in the lock mechanism, but it's free now.'

'Thanks. You're right, it's not a good night to be stuck out here. I'll be glad to get inside the inn and warm up a bit.'

It had been a relief to come across this place, to see the green-painted board displayed, with gold lettering offering bed and breakfast. There were vacancies, according to the sign, and she had made up her mind to stop and see what was available. What she could see of the inn looked clean and well kept, with tubs of flowers and brightly decked window-boxes that were lit up briefly by the intermittent flashes of lightning.

'Shall I carry your bag for you? It looks as though it might be heavy.'

'No, but thanks all the same. I'll manage fine now. You've been a great help.'

He smiled. 'You're welcome.' The smile relaxed his features and made him appear roguishly attractive at the same time.

He was watching her with a faint look of curiosity and she realised that she must have been staring. She pulled herself together and made an attempt to focus on matters in hand. She was tired and hungry and obviously not concentrating her attention on what she was doing. What she needed was to get herself back on track with a plate of wholesome food and a good night's sleep.

He closed the boot for her, and as thunder rumbled ominously in the distance he turned back to her with a frown.

'We're going to get soaked,' he remarked. 'Come on, let's get out of this rain.'

That sounded like a good idea, and Jassie hurried along beside him, giving in when he took the holdall from her because it was slowing her down. As they reached the main door, he laid his palm on the curve of her back to usher her inside the hotel, a feather-light touch but one that she registered with a gentle flood of warmth through her veins. He was a man who liked to be in control, she guessed, one who would lead the way.

'You look as though you're planning on staying here for a while,' he murmured, putting the holdall down in the carpeted entrance hall. 'Are you here on holiday?'

She shook her head, brushing the tumbled, damp curls from her cheek once more. He had a wonderfully rich voice, deep and sensual in the way that it smoothed over her.

'I was just passing through on my way further south,' she told him, 'but driving was getting treacherous, so I decided to stop here and book a room for the night.'

It would have been comforting to reach the little Cornish village where she was headed before nightfall, but there was no rush to get there and, all things considered, she felt it would be safer to stop here until the weather improved. Her interview at the Riverside Medical Centre wasn't until lunchtime tomorrow, so she would have plenty of time to find her way there and get herself organised.

'Seems like a sensible idea on a night like this. It's

not bad here,' he murmured. 'I've stayed here occasionally, and I think you'll find that the rooms are clean and comfortable, and the food's always very good.'

'I can't wait to sample it.' She bent to pick up her bag. 'I'll go and register at the desk, and get myself sorted out. I hope they're still serving dinner,' she added ruefully.

'I expect you'll be all right for an hour or so yet. The dining room's just across the hall.' He waved a hand towards a set of glass-paned doors to her right, and when she looked over there she saw that waiters were busy serving at the tables. That was encouraging.

Her glance strayed around the foyer. On the opposite side of the entrance hall, through a wide archway, she could see what must be the bar lounge. A dozen or so people were chatting quietly over drinks, comfortable and relaxed in the early evening, and her gaze was drawn to the large fireplace, where logs were burning, yellow and orange flames shooting upwards, flickering brightly. It was a heart-warming sight.

She gave him a smile and said brightly, 'Thank you for all your help, you've been very kind.'

'It was nothing,' he murmured, then added, 'I don't know your name...'

'It's Jassie—short for Jasmine,' she told him with a laugh, 'but nobody ever calls me that. Thanks again...' She looked up at him enquiringly.

'Alex,' he supplied. 'Alex Beaufort. Well...I'd better go and catch up with my friends and leave you to get yourself dried off.'

She nodded, watching him walk over to the bar and

join a group of men who were gathered there. They looked somehow like fishermen, wearing thick, knitted sweaters and dark trousers, and they obviously knew him because they greeted him cheerfully, and he was soon drawn deep into conversation with them.

Alex didn't look like a fisherman, though. He was tough and strong enough, but his skin didn't have the weathered look of his friends. Instead, it was lightly bronzed, and there was a faint shadowing along his jaw, which probably meant that he would need to shave again before too long. His clothes were casual but smart, certainly not the sort of thing you'd wear for hauling in nets.

Anyway, she decided, giving herself a mental shake, she ought not to be wasting time standing around thinking about someone she would probably never meet again after today. There were more important things to be getting on with...like finding herself a room for the night. She went over to the desk.

'Yes, I can let you have a room,' the landlord said in reply to her query. He was a weathered, friendly Cornishman, and Jassie felt at ease with him straight away. 'We're not too busy this early in the season. Have you come far?'

'From London. I was heading towards Land's End, but I thought better of going on when the weather changed for the worse.'

'On holiday, are you?'

Jassie shook her head. 'No, I'm planning on working down here.'

'Oh? Do you have something particular in mind?'

'I'm a doctor,' she explained. 'I have to go for an interview tomorrow.'

She already had the offer of a job, in fact, in a general practice not too far away from here. They were waiting for her to let them know if she would accept it, but she had told them she didn't want to commit herself until she had been for this interview. She wanted to take a look at the Riverside Medical Centre before she made up her mind what to do.

'I'll wish you luck, then. Do you think this place you're going to tomorrow might be what you want?'

'It might be. It's a semi-rural practice, near to the coast, and it sounds as though it might be a real change from what I've been used to in the city.'

Dr Hampton, the senior partner there, had written her a very friendly letter, inviting her down here for an informal interview, and from what he had said the surgery sounded like a warm and happy place to work.

'Do you know the area?' The landlord slid a book across the counter, and she signed in.

She nodded. 'Most of my family live around these parts, though it's been a few years since I was here for any length of time. I'm looking forward to being back.' It would be good to be close to her parents again after working for the last few years in the city. She had never cared much for city life, but she had done a good deal of her training in London and a job had come up there when she'd qualified. It was Rob's home, too, where he and his family lived, and because they had planned a future together, she had stayed.

For a moment or two, her gaze was troubled as she remembered what had happened. That phase of her life was behind her now, though. The engagement was off, and when she'd finally come to terms with it she'd had to acknowledge that what she'd felt deep down had been simply a kind of relief.

'Perhaps I'll make better headway tomorrow when the storm dies down.'

'It'll have caught a few on the hop, I dare say. It's a fierce one, this, and even worse out at sea. The spring tides can be tricky,' he added, pulling a face. 'If you stand in the back yard, you can hear the sea pounding on the harbour wall with a vengeance.' He sent a glance towards the fishermen in the bar. 'Those poor folks are lucky to have come out of it safely. It's definitely not a good night to be out there.'

Jassie frowned, wondering what they had been through, but before she could ask he reached behind him and unhooked a key from the board. 'Room number twelve,' he told her, passing it across the bar to her. 'I expect you'll want to go and take a look at it. Up the stairs and turn right. Then, if it suits you, you can come back down here and we'll fix you up with a good meal.'

'Thanks, I'll do that.'

'Do you want someone to show you the way and help with your bags?'

'No, it's all right. I'll manage.'

Upstairs, she wandered along the corridor, checking the numbers on the doors, and came across a young woman who was doing much the same thing.

She was a pretty, dark-haired girl, but she looked exhausted, and she was carrying a sleeping child who couldn't have been much more than eighteen months old. The child stirred and fidgeted, and his mother swayed a little so that Jassie reached out instinctively to offer her a helping hand.

'Are you all right?' she asked gently, observing the lines of fatigue in the young woman's face and noting the wince of pain that she gave as she shifted her arm to accommodate the restless child.

The woman nodded. 'I think so... At least, I shall be, once I get into my room.' She pushed her key into the lock, but as the child yawned and stretched in her arms, she bit her lip and let go of the key, and Jassie watched as most of the colour drained from her face.

'Let me give you a hand,' Jassie said, opening the door for her. 'You look as though you're in pain. Have you hurt yourself?'

'It's my wrist. I don't know what's the matter with it, but it's beginning to hurt a lot.'

'Would you like me to have a look at it? I'm a doctor...Jassie Radcliffe. I might be able to do something to help.'

The woman looked relieved. 'Would you?'

'Of course. Let's get you both inside.' Jassie ushered her into the room and settled her in a chair, gently taking the little boy from her arms and laying him down on the large divan bed. He mumbled in his sleep, not happy at being disturbed, then settled back on the pillow with a sigh, his silky hair falling softly over his flushed cheeks.

'He's well away, isn't he?' Jassie commented lightly, smiling down at him as she carefully tucked a corner of the duvet around him.

'It's a good thing he is, considering the day we've

had.' His mother gave him a tired but fond look, adding, 'He's usually into everything—ever since he could toddle he's been like a whirlwind, always on the go, racing around from one thing to the next, until he eventually runs out of steam close to bedtime. They say boys are more trouble than girls, don't they? Sam's definitely trouble and a half!'

She looked up at Jassie, who was laying her medical bag on the bed. 'I'm Sarah. I'm really glad you came along when you did, or I might still be struggling out there now. I thought I'd be all right on my own, but Sam was getting heavy, and then I realised how much my wrist and hand were throbbing.'

'I'm sure you'd have managed somehow,' Jassie murmured. 'Let me have a look at your wrist. Can you tell me what happened?'

'I'm not exactly sure what I did to it,' Sarah said. 'We were spending the day on a friend's yacht... The weather was fine to begin with, but then the storm blew up and we had to call the coastguard because we lost control and went aground. We were being thrown all over the place, and I must have done something to the wrist then.'

'It sounds as though you were lucky to get away with just a hurt wrist.'

'I was. I came out of it well by comparison with the others on board. My brother cracked some ribs and punctured his lung. He was in a really bad way until the lifeboat came along. The doctor put in a tube to reinflate the lung. Then one of the lifeboat crew broke an arm and the doctor said both men needed to go to hospital, so they were winched off the yacht by helicopter and taken there. My sister-in-law went with them, but the lifeboat crew took the rest of us off and brought us here.'

'That must have been scary for you.' Jassie looked up from her examination with a frown.

'It was. Things got really desperate on the boat, and I've never been so frightened in my life. All the time I was trying to keep hold of Sam here. We all had life-jackets on, but even so I was terrified that something would happen to him. Then I was thrown against the cabin wall, and I suppose I must have wrenched my wrist when I tried to steady myself. With all the worry about what was happening I didn't pay too much attention to it at the time, but it's beginning to hurt quite badly now.'

'Well, the good news is, I don't think anything's broken,' Jassie said, 'though you could get it X-rayed tomorrow just to be on the safe side. It would be more swollen if there was a fracture, and you would have more difficulty with movement. I think you've just sprained it. I can put a support bandage on it for you, if you like, and you could take paracetamol for the pain.'

Sarah nodded. 'I think I've got some in my bag.' She searched for them with her free hand, and would have stood up if Jassie hadn't stayed her with a hand on her shoulder.

'You sit tight while I fetch you something to drink.'

She went into the bathroom and came back with a glass of water. 'Swallow the tablets down, and I'll strap up the wrist for you.'

The bandaging only took a minute or two, and when

she had finished she said, 'There, that should make you feel more comfortable.'

'It feels much better already. Thanks. It's such a relief to have it bound up.'

'Good. I'm glad I could help. Is there anything more I can do for you?' Jassie perched on the edge of the bed and looked around. 'Do you have everything you need?'

'I'll be fine now, thanks. I'll rest for a bit, and then I might go downstairs to get something to eat, once I'm sure that Sam is all right. The landlord said there was a listening service I could use.'

'Are you just staying here just for the night?'

Sarah nodded. 'Yes. It was too late to make for home, and I thought we would be better off here. Tomorrow I can head straight for the hospital to see for myself how my brother's bearing up. They were a bit noncommittal when I rang...they just said he was comfortable.'

'I'm sure he must be out of any immediate danger since the doctor attended to him on board the yacht, and he'll be well looked after now. Try not to worry.' Jassie closed her medical bag and stood up. 'I'll leave you to it, then,' she said with a smile. 'I'm in room twelve if you need me in the next few minutes. After that, I'll be going downstairs to get myself something to eat.'

Jassie went to find her room, which, it turned out, was further along the corridor and around the corner, down a short flight of steps. She battled with the worn lock and gave a sigh of relief when it finally gave way and the door opened up into her room. Putting her bags down on the floor, she looked around. The carpet was a deep plum shade, soft underfoot, and the room was simply furnished and pleasing on the eye.

The bedcovers were a delicate blend of dusky pink roses and pale sprigged leaves on a background of cream, with curtains and shades to match, and when she tried out the bed, it felt good, springy and comfortable.

There wasn't time to lie down and relax just now, though, because she really wanted to take a few minutes to quickly freshen up. Slipping her damp jacket onto a hanger, she washed her face and hands and made use of the hair-dryer that was on the dresser. She tried to tease the wayward copper-coloured curls that framed her face into some kind of order, but in the end she had to be satisfied that at least her hair was healthily clean and softly shining. Ready at last, she went downstairs to eat.

A table had been set aside for her in a corner of the dining room and she sat down and ordered lasagne and a pot of tea. While she was waiting for the food to be brought to her she took the letter from Dr Hampton out of her bag and read it through once more.

The Riverside sounded like just the kind of place where she could find her feet after being in London. What she needed was a change of scene, something totally different, and the more she read the letter the more she felt that she was coming home.

A waiter brought her the food she had ordered, and she put the letter to one side and savoured every mouthful, finishing off her meal with a satisfying helping of apple pie and whipped cream. Replete at last, she felt as though she was slowly beginning to wind down and, stifling a yawn, she got to her feet and started to head for her room.

As she crossed the foyer, she caught a glimpse of Sarah in the bar lounge among the group of men Jassie had seen earlier, and now she wondered if they were the crew of the lifeboat. Sarah was talking to Alex, but he looked up just then and excused himself, making his way towards Jassie.

'Jassie...' He was frowning, and she slowed down, wondering what was on his mind.

'Is something wrong?'

'Not wrong, exactly. It's just that Sarah was telling me about her wrist. She said you took a look at it for her.'

Jassie shrugged lightly. 'She was in pain, so I offered to help out, that's all. Is there a problem?'

'Not a problem, as such...but since I'm Sarah's doctor, I would rather you had sent her to me instead of trying to treat her yourself. I should have been the one who looked after her.'

That was one query solved, at least. She had known he wasn't a fisherman like the others, hadn't she? Though he must have been out on the lifeboat with them. Still, doctor or not, it didn't give him the right to have a go at her over what had been a simple gesture of human kindness, did it?

Jassie raised a delicately arched brow. 'If I had known you were her doctor, of course I would have referred her to you...but she didn't mention it, so I don't see how I could have done so.'

'You could have asked her if she planned on seeing her doctor about it.'

'That's true, except that her injury happened out of surgery hours, and I doubt she would have wanted to spend hours in Casualty, waiting to be attended to. Anyway, there was nothing to stop her from asking you to examine her...but perhaps she didn't want to trouble you? I did suggest that she have it X-rayed.'

'So she said.'

'I hope she's feeling a bit more comfortable now,' Jassie added abruptly. She could see that he was still annoyed.

'I'm sure she is. Even so, perhaps you'll bear in mind what I've said next time a situation like this arises.' He was frowning again, and Jassie wondered if he was about to find some other fault with her.

Suddenly she decided that she'd had enough. It had been a long day, and she was in no mood for a protracted discussion on medical ethics.

'It's getting late,' she murmured smoothly. 'I think I'll go up to my room now. If you'll excuse me?'

His eyes narrowed, but he obviously thought better of saying any more, because instead he stepped aside and nodded, saying coolly, 'Goodnight, then.'

'Goodnight.'

It was only when she was back in her room that it occurred to her that he might not have realised that she was a doctor. If Sarah hadn't mentioned it, he could have believed that Jassie was just an amateur, practising a bit of first aid.

Whatever...she wasn't going to let it trouble her any longer. Instead, she ran a bath for herself and relaxed in the fragrant bubbles for a while, soaking away the tensions of the day. From tomorrow, she would have a clearer idea of what she wanted to do with her life from now on. She would have a fresh start, a new beginning, and she was looking forward to that.

Getting out of the bath a while later, she dried herself and slid a short cotton nightshirt over her head, smoothing it absently down over her thighs while she thought over her plans for the morning. Perhaps she ought to get the map out and have a look at exactly where the Riverside Centre was situated. That way, she could set off after breakfast tomorrow and be on her way without any delay. The address was on the letter from Dr Hampton.

Oh, no...the letter... A flash of memory surfaced, and she remembered that she had been reading it at the table in the dining room, but she didn't recall pushing it back into her bag. Had she left it down there? The waiter had arrived with the food and she had forgotten all about it.

She went over to the dresser and rummaged in her handbag, but the letter wasn't there. There was nothing for it—she would have to go downstairs and fetch it. With any luck, it would still be on the table.

She quickly put on a wrap, slipped her room key into the pocket and made for the dining room. At this time of night, no one would be around to see her.

Thankfully, the letter was on the table where she had left it, and she guessed the waiter had realised that she would come back down for it. Pushing it into her pocket, she turned back to the stairs.

The lights in the corridors were dimmed now, and

everything looked strange and shadowy as she made her way along the darkened passageway. This place was a maze of corridors and staircases, and her room was in a little annexe around a corner of the building. Yawning tiredly, she reached in her pocket for her key.

Scanning the doors, she found number twelve and inserted the key in the lock. It gave her trouble, as before, but she persevered, manoeuvring it patiently and rattling it sharply when it refused to give way. Getting vexed after a while, she gave the door a hefty push, hoping that would shake things up a bit, and suddenly it gave way. The door swung wide and she fell into the room and made a soft collision with something...a living, breathing something.

Stunned, and momentarily out of breath, she blinked and tried to absorb the shock of what was happening.

'What the...?'

The male voice sounded perplexed and just as startled as she was, but Jassie was too dumbfounded to make any attempt at an answer. Her fingers tangled with warm, smooth skin, and a hard ribcage, and as she dazedly looked up, she encountered mesmerising gold-flecked eyes and realised with a shock that the man she was desperately clutching was Alex Beaufort.

Her glance shimmered over him and she saw that he was bare-chested, his hair wet and spiky, and he had a towel fastened firmly around his hips. She caught the drift of a faint musky fragrance, essentially male and compelling to the senses.

All at once her fingers burned as she registered the heat emanating from his naked flesh, and her whole body sizzled as the intimacy of her situation dawned on her. Her breasts were gently crushed against him, her thighs were in heated contact with his, and just thinking about what was happening was making her feel hot and dizzy.

She struggled to regain her balance, and Alex's hands went to her shoulders, steadying her at last, so that eventually the world stopped spinning. She stared up at him with wide blue eyes.

'What...what are you doing here?'

His mouth made a wry slant. 'I could ask you the same thing. I don't recall ordering room service.' He flicked a glance down over her slender form and her cheeks heated as she discovered that her wrap had loosened in the fray. Her thin nightshirt was short enough to be scarcely decent and was slit down each side to show a smooth expanse of naked thigh.

His gaze lingered on the shapely line of her legs and he murmured softly, 'Not that I'm complaining, you understand.'

Indignation sparked in her blue eyes. Was he actually making fun of her? As if it wasn't bad enough that she was in this predicament in the first place.

'I don't know what you're talking about...' she managed to splutter. She was all too conscious that she was wearing next to nothing, without him drawing attention to it. And as for him...

She averted her eyes from the naked expanse of bronzed chest and the towel that hugged his hips. What did he think he was doing, helping himself to her shower?

'You still haven't answered my question,' she said tautly, drawing the wrap firmly around herself and straightening her shoulders. 'What are you doing in my room?'

A dark brow arched. '*Your* room?'

'That's what I said. This is number twelve, isn't it? I distinctly remember seeing that it was the right number. I had my key in the lock—'

'And I heard someone trying to get in and wondered what on earth was going on, so I pulled the door open.' His mouth twisted. 'If I'd known you were going to drop in, I'd have put the champagne on ice.'

Jassie drew in a deep breath. 'This may seem funny to you,' she said in a strained tone, 'but I'd like to get to bed at some point tonight—' She broke off as amusement gleamed in his eyes and he opened the door wider and waved a hand towards the double divan behind him.

'By all means. Come in. Be my guest.'

She bit back a sharp retort and stared beyond him at the deep blue quilt that covered the bed, and then slowly let her gaze wander about the room. Blue curtains, blue shades, a grey flecked carpet. Her jaw dropped.

'I thought...I thought this was my room. Number twelve. I don't understand...'

'It is number twelve,' Alex said pleasantly. 'Twelve A. I think you'll find that you're next door.' He pointed to the adjacent door.

'Oh,' she said in a small voice. 'I didn't realise... I'm sorry. It...it must be the lighting up here.' She was flustered, and her words were coming faster than was sensible and were tripping over themselves. 'I'm really very sorry.'

'Don't worry about it,' he said with a faint smile. 'It's been a long day for all of us.'

'Yes...yes, that must be it.' She backed away, and retreated hastily into the corridor. 'I'll...I'll leave you in peace, then.'

She turned away so that he wouldn't see the hot colour flaring in her cheeks, and concentrated her attention on getting her key in the correct lock. She had made an utter fool of herself.

Her only hope was that she had seen the last of Alex Beaufort, that she wouldn't bump into him in the morning and that she would eventually be able to push the whole sorry incident to the back of her mind.

CHAPTER TWO

JASSIE took her time going down to breakfast next morning, figuring that if she delayed long enough there was a good chance Alex would have left the inn already and she might avoid running into him. It made her hot all over to even think about what had happened last night.

When she finally headed towards the stairs, she saw that Sarah's door was open, and Sarah was just coming out of her room, looking harassed.

'Come on, Sam,' she was saying in a coaxing tone. 'We'll go and get something to eat.'

'Bekfust?' the little boy said.

'That's right. Breakfast.'

Jassie stopped to say hello, and Sarah turned to her in relief.

'Oh,' she said, with a quick smile, 'You're still here. I thought you would have left already. We're running so late. I can't get Sam to co-operate with me this morning.'

She held out a hand to the little boy, who looked shyly up at Jassie, and then edged into the safety of his mother's skirt and peered out at her from behind the folds of material. His cheeks were flushed, and Jassie thought perhaps he was running a cold. 'For some reason, he's dragging his feet this morning.'

'Perhaps he feels odd, waking up in a strange place,'

Jassie murmured, 'and yesterday could have been a bit frightening for him. I expect he'll feel better about things as the day goes on.' Bearing in mind what Alex had said the previous evening, she hoped Sarah wouldn't ask her to examine him.

'You're probably right,' Sarah agreed, then added, 'Shall we have breakfast together?'

'Good idea.'

There was no sign of Alex as they started breakfast, and when the landlord proffered the information that all of the other overnight guests had left early, Jassie was relieved enough to relax and enjoy her meal.

'Will you be going home as soon as you've finished eating?' she asked Sarah. 'It must have been disruptive for you, having to stay here overnight.'

'I shan't go straight away,' Sarah murmured, between efforts to coax Sam to eat. 'I want to go and see my brother in hospital, just to make sure that he's doing all right. They took him to the local general hospital, so it isn't too far away for me to visit.'

'Oh, that's good. It will make things much easier for you. I hope you find that he's feeling better.'

When they had finished eating, Jassie went to settle her bill and then said her goodbyes to Sarah and Sam before she went out to her car.

She had a couple of hours to finish her journey to the village and find the Riverside Health Centre. That should be ample time for her to get her bearings.

The air was fresh this morning, now that the sunshine had cleared the rain, and the drive was a pleasant one, taking her along country roads where the hedgerows were beginning to green up and cherry trees were showing the first signs of budding blossom.

She found the surgery easily enough. It was part of a rambling stone-built house, set back from the road and surrounded by mature trees and shrubs, which gave it a mellowed, homely appeal. Jassie breathed in the clean air, and thought with satisfaction how different this was from the city. She could see herself working here.

Looking about her as she walked along the wide path, she approached the main door and went inside.

'Oh, hello, Dr Radcliffe,' the receptionist greeted her when she had introduced herself. 'We were expecting you. If you'd like to take a seat in the coffee-lounge, I'll let Dr Hampton know you're here. Come along with me and I'll show you the way.'

'Thanks.' Left alone in the lounge, Jassie pulled in a deep breath and made herself stay calm. It was just an interview, and nothing to get uptight about.

Dr Hampton came into the room a few minutes later, and greeted her with a smile. He was in his late fifties or early sixties, a kindly looking man, with light brown hair which had been faded by the sun and was streaked with grey. He held out a hand to her.

'Dr Radcliffe, it's good to see you.'

'And you.'

'I'm just glad you managed to get here safely,' he said. 'I know you had to travel all the way from London. Can I offer you a cup of coffee?'

'No, thank you. I'm fine.'

'All right, then, if you're sure, we'll make a start, and I'll show you around the place. There should have been three of us to greet you today, but Dr Wiseman has had to go out on a call, and my partner is busy for the moment, seeing a patient. The fellow came by on the off-chance that one of us might be able to see him at the last minute.' He led her to the door. 'The poor man was having terrible chest pains, so we couldn't ask him to come back later.'

There were four surgeries, a couple of treatment rooms, where minor procedures were carried out, and a separate wing at the side of the house where the health visitors held their clinics. Jassie was immediately taken by the spaciousness of the place and the welcoming atmosphere that had been created, with comfortable furniture, magazine tables and plants, and bright corners where children could play.

'It's much bigger than I expected,' she told Dr Hampton, as they looked into each room, and when he showed her the modern equipment they had installed, she was impressed. They talked generally as he showed her around, and Jassie found that they got on well together, and he was more than happy to answer her questions. He was a man that she felt she could work with amicably, and it was only after they had finished the tour and were on their way back to the coffee-lounge that she realised he had probably been subtly interviewing her the whole time.

One of the surgeries had been occupied as they'd made the tour, and now, as they passed by it, the door opened and a man came out, clutching a prescription.

He turned in the doorway and said to the doctor in the room beyond, 'Thanks for seeing me at such short notice. I didn't know what was happening to me at the time. It was pretty scary, thinking I was having a heart attack, but it feels much easier now.'

Jassie heard the murmured reply, 'I'm glad I could help. Any time you're worried, come in and see me.'

That deep, gravel-edged voice had a disturbingly familiar ring to it, and for a moment she was too taken aback to do anything more than stand to one side and look on while the patient turned around and exchanged a few words with Dr Hampton.

A moment later, the surgery door opened wider and as the doctor came out into the corridor Jassie's blue eyes widened, a tide of heat sweeping along her cheekbones.

He stood very still for a moment, looking at her. Then, 'Hello, Jassie,' Alex Beaufort said, his dark brows lifting in surprise. 'What are you doing here? You're not ill, are you?'

She stared at him, her lips parting a little in sheer astonishment. Her glance took in the beautifully tailored grey suit he was wearing, the immaculate shirt with perfectly laundered collar and crisp-looking cuffs that slipped back to reveal strong wrists and hands. He was holding an envelope that she assumed contained the patient's notes.

She realised he was waiting for an answer. 'I... N-no, I'm fine, thank you.' She was vaguely aware of the patient finishing his conversation with Dr Hampton and making his way towards the exit but, other than that, her mind was in a whirl.

'What's this? Do you two know each other?' Dr Hampton asked, intrigued, glancing from one to the other.

'We met yesterday at the Harbour Inn,' Alex explained. 'Jassie was held up by the storm and had to spend the night there.'

'And you,' Jassie added faintly, still in a state of shock from seeing him there, 'were with the lifeboat crew. I'd assumed you worked at a surgery further north.' Even as she said it, a fluttery sensation of doubt was starting up in her stomach.

He shook his head. 'I went out with the lifeboat, but not from the northern station. I went from here. As soon as we received the call that a boat was in distress the crew called me out to attend to the injured. Because we're so near to the coast, that's part of our role here at the Riverside, to be on call for the lifeboat whenever we're needed. A helicopter was on its way to the scene, but they needed us as back-up.'

She pulled in a sharp breath. 'But what were you doing so far off course? Why didn't the lifeboat return to its own port?'

'The conditions were too bad last night, and it would have been too dangerous to navigate through the rocks offshore. It sometimes happens that they have to put in for the night somewhere else and return home when the sea is calmer.'

'I didn't know that. I suppose I'd naturally assumed that you belonged in that region.'

Alex's mouth twisted, and she grimaced inwardly, just knowing that he was remembering how she had got her bearings wrong last night and believed he'd been in the wrong room. The whole sorry incident reared up to taunt her once again. Oh, how she wished she hadn't made that decision to stop at the inn last night.

He cut in on her wayward thoughts. 'So…if you're not here about your health…?'

'Alex,' Dr Hampton said easily, 'Dr Radcliffe is here to be interviewed for the job.'

'Dr Radcliffe?' Alex echoed, clearly startled. He slanted a glance over her from head to toe, taking in her neat outfit, a trim suit with narrow skirt that flattered her long legs and a jacket that nipped in at the waist to emphasise her slender figure.

Perhaps he was reassessing her. He had seen her at her worst yesterday, bedraggled from the rain, but today she was much more businesslike and professional. She had pinned up her hair so that the abundance of curls was more or less tamed for once, with just a few spiralling tendrils escaping to soften the oval of her face.

'I had no idea,' he said at last, 'though perhaps I should have guessed from the way you strapped up Sarah's wrist that you knew what you were about.' He frowned. 'At the time I thought you had just taken it on yourself to do it for her.'

She had guessed as much, but if he'd thought she'd made a decent job of it, why had he bothered to complain?

'I did what I thought was best,' she said calmly. 'After all, last night was a little unusual, all things considered.'

'It certainly was,' he said with a wry smile and a glint in his eye. 'There was a fair amount of confusion all round.'

He was doing it deliberately, she decided, trying to get under her skin and remind her of things she would rather have forgotten. 'What I'm trying to say,' she said stiffly, 'is that under normal circumstances things would have been very different. I wouldn't have needed to treat her, and she would have come here to see you.'

'Maybe. Of course, the problem with that is that things around here are very often *not* quite the norm,' Alex said drily. 'That's why we have a duty rota to be on call for the lifeboat station. And when we're not helping out with hazards at sea, there are the tourists to deal with. It's amazing what kind of mishaps they can get themselves into. That's why the practice needs to take on someone who can deal competently with any eventuality.'

Was he saying that he didn't think that she was suitable for the job? Jassie frowned. How would he have come by that decision already? And if that was the case, she couldn't accept his hasty judgement of her. He didn't know her at all, did he? After all, they had only met the night before!

'I'm sure I could handle all manner of emergencies, even those at sea,' she defended herself. 'I've worked in accident and emergency as well as a lot of other areas of medicine that are useful in general practice. You wouldn't need to worry that I won't pull my weight.'

'Have you worked on boats before?'

'Well, no…not exactly, but, then, how many people have? I can't see that it would bother me. I can adapt to most circumstances.'

'I'm sure you would do your best,' he said agreeably enough, but to her finely tuned sensitivities his tone implied that her best simply wouldn't be good enough.

She sent him a querying look, and he added carefully, 'You saw what happened to Sarah yesterday. The conditions were bad out at sea in the storm, and she was flung across the cabin and hurt her arm in the process. You and she are of a similar build, both of you are slim and fairly petite. Do you really think that you would physically be able to cope?'

Jassie's chin lifted. She had to make him see that she was a capable and thoroughly competent doctor. 'Have you forgotten that Sarah's brother was injured, too?' she murmured. 'Cracked ribs, I think she said, and one of the lifeboat crew came out of it badly, too. I hardly think their physical strength stood for much in the circumstances, so I don't see that your argument stands.'

'From what Dr Radcliffe was telling me,' Dr Hampton interceded, 'she had a long stint at one of London's busiest casualty departments. Her references make it clear that she's had to work under pressure a great deal, and the consultant who headed her team is full of praise for the way she handled things. She told me a little about her work in specialist areas—paediatrics, gynaecology and obstetrics. They would be very useful to us.'

'You've had some time to get to know each other, then?' Alex murmured.

'Oh, yes. While you were busy with Jim Henderson,

I took the opportunity to show her around, and we were able to have a good chat.'

'I'm sure that must have been enlightening,' Alex said, his mouth making a faint quirk. 'I wish I'd been there.' He looked along the corridor. 'Are you on your way to the coffee-lounge now?' At his partner's nod, he wafted the envelope he was holding and said, 'I just need to go and give these notes to Carole in Reception so that she can file them away, and I'll be with you both in a minute.'

When he joined them in the room a short time later, he seated himself so that he was directly facing Jassie, and there followed a half an hour of interrogation that delved into every aspect of her career so far. He wasn't making anything easy for her, and that made Jassie all the more determined to keep her cool and answer every question with thoughtful consideration. It was Dr Hampton, in the end, who called a halt.

'I think Dr Beaufort and I would like a few minutes to talk to each other alone,' he said. 'You'll appreciate that we've seen several candidates already over the last day or two, and we need to go over some of the points that we've covered. Bear with us for just a little longer, will you?' He smiled and added, 'I'll ask Carole to bring you some coffee while you're waiting.'

'Thank you.' After that grilling from Alex, she felt as though she could do with it.

The two men left her alone to mull over things while they went to Dr Hampton's room, and Jassie felt her confidence ebbing away with every minute that passed. On the surface, Alex's questioning had seemed straightforward enough, but she was intuitive enough to catch the subtle undertones and she knew that he was still not convinced about her suitability for this job. That bothered her a lot, because the more she learned about the Riverside, the more she wanted to work here.

She straightened her shoulders as the door opened once more, and Dr Hampton came over to her.

'Dr Radcliffe,' he said with a smile. 'We'd like to offer you the job...you understand about the six months' trial period, don't you? It gives both sides time to get to know each other and will give you the chance to make a decision as to whether you're happy with the way things are.' He searched her face to gauge her reaction. 'What do you say—will you take it?'

Delight bubbled up and fizzed inside her, and then belatedly she remembered that he was waiting for an answer. 'I'd like to accept, very much,' she murmured. 'Thank you.'

He cupped her hand in his and grinned. 'I'm very glad of that.' Behind him, she caught sight of Alex's somewhat taut expression, and she could only begin to guess how much pressure Dr Hampton had exerted to make him accept his decision. She didn't doubt for one minute that it had been the senior partner's will that had won the day.

'You made an excellent candidate,' Dr Hampton was saying. 'We need a woman doctor here, you know, and we're convinced you'll make an excellent addition to our team.'

'I'll do my best to live up to your expectations,' she managed huskily.

Dr Hampton beamed a smile at her. 'Now, my dear, to practical matters. Have you given any thought to where you might be going to live? Do you have any family around here, or have you left them all behind in London?'

'My parents were both born in Cornwall, and I have a brother and an aunt who both live locally.'

'Do you have just the one brother?'

'No, there are two of them. Steve lives around here, and Nick was working in London until recently.'

'Are you going to be living with your parents?'

Jassie shook her head. 'They live too far away from the surgery to make it a realistic proposition. I thought I might rent a property for the time being.'

'You don't have a particular place in mind, then?' Dr Hampton was thoughtful for a moment. 'There's a cottage not far from here, which might be to your liking. It has been empty for about a couple of weeks now. It belongs to the doctor who was here before you…Dr Marriott. Her husband's firm has transferred him up North on short notice, and so they've had to move out in a bit of a hurry. They've decided to rent out the cottage for the moment, on a six-month tenancy, though they're quite likely to consider an offer to buy at some time in the future. I believe the amount they're asking is quite reasonable—you might want to look the place over this afternoon, to see if it suits you.'

'That sounds like a good idea. I think I'll do that, if you could let me have directions.'

'I'll take you over there,' Alex said. 'It's not easy to find unless you know the way.'

She looked at him guardedly. 'Are you sure you don't mind doing that? Don't you have to be here for afternoon surgery?'

'We close one afternoon a week. Dr Hampton does a stint at the local hospital, and our other colleague, Alan Wiseman, and I take it in turns to be on call. I'm free this afternoon, so it's no bother at all. Besides, it's only a couple of miles from the surgery, and it's on my way home.'

He was being considerate, despite the fact that he probably didn't want her for this job, and she couldn't see any reason not to take him up on his offer. 'Thank you, then. I'd appreciate that.'

They set off for the cottage about a half an hour later, with Alex at the wheel of a smart-looking silver saloon and Jassie following in her more ancient runabout.

The lanes were narrow and winding, taking her through a beautiful wooded valley towards a small cove that she glimpsed intermittently along the way. The sea was a startling blue-green, tranquil today so that you would never have suspected it could ever turn treacherous.

The cottage was part way up a hillside track, hidden amongst early-flowering shrubs and tall trees so that she came upon it slowly. Straight away liked what she saw. Stone-built, like the surgery, it had a rustic appeal, with a steeply angled thatched roof that was echoed in the smaller thatched porch. Georgian-style windows peeped out from under rounded eaves, and around the front door there was a rambling rose that would burst into full bloom in a few months' time.

'It's lovely,' she murmured, stepping out of the car onto the widely curving drive and breathing in the fresh sea air.

'It is, isn't it?' Alex came to stand beside her. 'If you look down from the fence over there, you get a good view of the bay.' He drew her towards the vantage point, his arm brushing hers as he pointed out the glittering sweep of the ocean.

She drew in a quick breath, but it wasn't simply the beautiful scene that had taken the air from her lungs. It was his nearness, the lightest drift of his fingers against her hand which had caused her senses to shift up a gear, leaving her shaken and oddly off balance. How was it that such a simple gesture could make her so vitally aware of him? Perhaps the events of last night were still too firmly embedded in her mind.

'This is one of the prettiest places in Cornwall,' he said, 'a sleepy little village where nothing much stirs. A big change from what you're used to, I'll bet.'

'A change from the city, yes,' she said with feeling. 'Where I lived it was mainly built up, with bus stops right near your door and the traffic waking you from early in the morning.'

'You'll not find that here. It's very quiet in this neck of the woods. I dare say you'll find it a complete contrast to begin with. In the end, though, you could find that it's too peaceful.'

'Meaning you think I'm a city girl and I'm only down here for a short spell?' She looked at him quizzically. 'You really don't have any faith in me at all, do you?'

'If you want my honest opinion...no, I don't. I don't

think you'll be able to handle this job. No matter what you say to the contrary, I believe physical strength matters when you're out on the lifeboats. It's not everything, but it gives you more control over what happens.'

'The doctor I'm replacing is a woman,' Jassie pointed out. 'I didn't hear you expressing any doubts about her role in the practice.'

'She's a much more robust individual than you are. Besides, she very rarely went out on the lifeboat because Dr Hampton always took a turn. That's changing, and he won't be going out on a regular basis any more now that he's nearing retirement.'

'I'm not going to be able to convince you, simply by telling you that I can cope, am I? The only way I'll be able to do that is to show you.'

'That wasn't my only reason for doubt,' Alex said bluntly. 'I also think you're young and relatively inexperienced, and I would have preferred to take on someone who had a few more years behind them. Besides, I'm not convinced this is the kind of place you really want to work in. We see a lot of tourists, people who are only here for a very short time, and yet you say you're looking for the kind of practice where you can get to know your patients.'

'Tourists only make up a part of your list,' Jassie objected. 'That's one of the reasons I'm drawn to the Riverside. There's the possibility of so much variety in the work.'

'You say that now, when you've just come down from London and a seaside practice has a lot of appeal. Perhaps, right now, you want a break, a holiday by the sea to refresh you, but I think after a while you'll be hankering for the city lights again.'

'Dr Hampton seems to be taking a different view,' she pointed out.

'That doesn't make him right. Dr Hampton is a good man, a gentle man, but completely out of touch with the reality of the situation. Out of deference to the fact that he's the senior partner, and he has the final say, I have to go along with him, but you'll have to do a lot to convince me that you belong here.'

'That's just what I intend to do,' Jassie said, determination lacing her voice. 'I'll show you that you're wrong about me. I can be every bit as valuable to the practice as you would wish. You'll see.'

She moved briskly in the direction of the front porch of the house, and threw back, 'Now, are you going to unlock this door and let me look around this place? I'd like to be able to see what it is that I'm getting.'

'You've made your decision already, then, have you?'

She nodded. 'Oh, yes...almost. I've fallen in love with the cottage just from the outside, and I can't believe that the inside won't be every bit as perfect. I can see myself living here already, looking out over the sea every day. Renting it will suit me fine for the moment.'

'Renting is probably for the best,' he agreed silkily. 'A six-month lease gives you room to manoeuvre. After all, you never know how things might turn out.'

'You're convinced that I'll scuttle back to London within a few months, aren't you?' she said with an edge to her voice.

'I think it's on the cards.'

She flashed him a challenging blue glance. Alex didn't know what she was capable of yet, but he would find out soon enough. 'Believe me,' she told him decisively, 'I'm not going anywhere.'

The look he gave her was sceptical. 'We'll see,' he said.

CHAPTER THREE

'IT MIGHT be helpful if you were to go with Alex on his rounds this week, Jassie,' Dr Hampton suggested a few days later. They were all assembled in the coffee-lounge for the early morning staff meeting, an established part of the working-day routine. 'That way, you'll get to know your way around more quickly.'

'Yes, of course I'll do that,' Jassie said, 'if Alex has no objection to having me with him. It's been a while since I lived in the area, and this particular region isn't familiar to me.'

'I've no problem with that,' Alex murmured.

'Good. That's settled, then.' John Hampton nodded, pleased. 'We've quite an area to cover here, with the villages scattered around and the coastal stretch, not to mention the more isolated farms. But you'll get used to it soon enough, and at least we have the summer ahead of us, which will make it easier for you to get about.'

'I expect it will.' In fact, she would have preferred to have kept some distance between herself and Alex for the time being, even if it had meant struggling to find her way around on her own, but she wasn't going to say that to anyone. Since the day of her interview, she had been on edge whenever Alex had been around, unable to shake off the feeling that she was on trial here…which she was, of course, as far as he was concerned.

John Hampton, on the other hand, appeared to take a much more relaxed attitude to the situation, and she felt sure that if it was left to him she would be accepted into the fold without a problem.

The meeting broke up a few minutes later, and Alex said briskly, 'It's a fairly short list this morning, but I'd like to get away as soon as you're ready.'

Jassie finished the last of her coffee and put down her cup. 'I'm ready now,' she murmured, getting to her feet.

'Good. We'll make a start, then.' He led the way out to his car, and filled her in on some of the details as they drove along.

For the most part, she discovered, the calls were fairly routine—a few viral infections, a man with bronchitis and a child who was suffering from a sickness bug. Alex was gentle and caring with all of his patients, and in turn they all seemed to know him and like him.

'I've left Martin Prentice until last,' Alex told her as they set off finally towards a village on the far side of the practice. 'That way, he'll have had more time to get himself sorted out this morning. He's quite an elderly man, and he has been suffering from Parkinson's disease for a few years now, so it takes him a while to get going. The tremors affect both sides of his body. So far we've managed to keep the symptoms under reasonable control through a mix of physiotherapy and treatment with levodopa.'

Jassie glanced down at the notepad in her lap and

checked the receptionist's written comments. 'Apparently, his wife called the surgery to ask if we would visit today. She said she was concerned about him, and she thought perhaps his condition was changing for the worse.'

'It could be. I imagine Jane must need reassurance almost as much as he does.'

Jane Prentice showed them into her sitting room a few minutes later. 'He didn't want me to bother you, but I made up my mind to call you anyway,' she confided. 'If he had his own way, he would just put up with things as they are, and I'm sure it isn't right for him to do that.'

Martin had been sitting in an armchair, but he got to his feet unsteadily when they came into the room. He was in his late sixties, white-haired, a man who would have been tall once but was stooped now, with visible trembling in his limbs.

'Hello, Martin,' Alex greeted him warmly. 'How are you today?'

'Oh, I'm not too bad,' Martin answered with a rueful grimace. 'It's just that I can't seem to get my feet to do what I want them to do, but that's how it is, you know. I didn't want Jane to go bothering you, but she would insist.'

Alex nodded. 'I'm glad she did. I can see that you're having some difficulty, and you should always let me know if you're not feeling too good. Let me examine you, and then we'll talk about what we can do for you.'

He was very thorough and, as Jassie had observed in their visits to other patients, he had a calm and understanding manner that helped to soothe the man, who was obviously going through a difficult time, albeit he was unwilling to admit it.

'I think it would be a good idea for you to take another drug alongside the one that you're used to,' Alex said after a while. 'It should help cut out some of the more major unwanted movements of your limbs and help you stay in control.'

'Do you really think it will work?' Martin asked doubtfully.

'I do. The combination is usually quite effective, so you should find it gives you some relief. We'll start you off on that today, and I'll check up on you again in a week's time. If you have any problems in the meantime, just ring the surgery and let me know. Don't leave it and suffer in silence.'

'Thanks, Doctor.' Martin looked relieved. 'I didn't realise there was any other treatment I could have. I must say, I feel a lot happier now, knowing that something can be done.'

'It's a good thing for you that Jane took no notice of your protests, then, and went ahead and called me anyway.'

Martin gave a wry smile. 'She's always been a tough one, my Jane. Waste of time, anything I say. She always goes and does her own thing in the end.'

They took their leave of the couple a few minutes later, and Jassie said as she slid into the passenger seat of Alex's car, 'I was reading about work on a new treatment of diseases like Parkinson's through gene therapy. There was talk of transplanting specialised cells to produce an improvement in the condition. It will be marvellous if something comes of it.'

'It certainly would,' Alex said, starting up the engine and manoeuvring the car back into the road. 'I think we'll find that medicine will change quite dramatically in the next decade or so. I dare say it will be a few years before anything comes of it, but I imagine there are all kinds of treatment that will spring from the work going on now. Until recently, scientists thought they knew which part of the brain was involved in Parkinson's, and now they've found another area which might be having an effect. It all helps to concentrate their research, doesn't it?'

On their way back to the surgery, they drove across a headland overlooking a wide bay, and he pointed out the huge waves that rolled in with the tide and broke on the beach in foaming white bands of surf.

'In the season you'd be hard pushed to find a space to call your own down there. People come with their wetsuits and surfboards and spend hours in the water.'

'Do you ever join them?'

'When I get the chance. There's no feeling like it, moving with the tide, feeling the swell beneath your feet and cresting the waves.'

She could imagine him pitting his wits against the power of the sea. He had the build for it, a supple strength that would lend itself to that kind of sport.

'What about you?' he asked. 'Have you tried surfing?'

Jassie shook her head. 'No, I haven't. I've watched people doing it, but it always looks to me as though it would take a lot of practice to get it right, and since

I don't get down to the coast that often, it isn't something I've taken up. Perhaps I'll have a go one day.'

The road they were on dipped down now towards the quay, and Alex slowed the car, negotiating a passage to the main road that would lead them back to the surgery.

They passed close by a man seated by the rail, an easel set up in front of him. Jassie couldn't see what materials he was using, but he was drawing portraits, and she guessed they were done with chalk.

The man was youngish, in his late twenties, and his build was so similar to that of her brother that she looked thoughtfully at him as they drove by.

'Something wrong?' Alex asked, sending her an oblique glance.

'No, nothing. It's just that the man we just drove past looked a bit like my brother.'

'Is your brother an artist?'

'It's his hobby, something he does in his spare time. He's very good, and he was thinking of taking it up professionally at one time, until my mother persuaded him that he needed to do something that would earn him a decent living.' She made a wry grimace. 'She was probably right—there's not much money in painting, unless you're famous. Anyway, he took her advice and took up research work instead.'

'Does he work around here?'

'No. He lives and works in the London area...or rather, he had a job there until recently. He resigned, took some leave that was owing to him and headed for Cornwall. I think Nick was planning on a month-long holiday down here, but so far he hasn't been home to see my parents. He promised that he would be in touch, but we haven't heard from him yet.'

'Is that a problem?'

'Not exactly. It's just that he had an argument with my fiancé some time ago, and it made things awkward between us for a while. I wanted to be able to let him know that it's all OK, that I don't blame him for anything, but he left before I had the chance to talk to him properly about it.'

'You have a fiancé back in London?' Alex's brows drew together in a frown.

She pulled in a deep breath as she thought back over what she had told him. 'Perhaps I should have said ex-fiancé. He and Nick worked together at a pharmaceutical company.'

'It's odd that you should miss off the "ex",' Alex suggested thoughtfully. 'Perhaps it was a Freudian slip?'

'Not really.' She pulled a face, acknowledging how it might have seemed. 'I wasn't thinking, that's all. My mind was on my brother, more than anything else. My relationship with Rob is definitely over. We were to have been married this summer, but we called it off.'

'I'm sorry.' He paused, watching her expression. 'Did the break-up happen a long time ago?'

'No...it was fairly recent, although I suppose it had been coming on for some time.' She winced. 'The signs had been there for some months. It's just that it took me a while to realise it.'

'And is that why you made up your mind to come

down here to work? Did you want to get away from the situation?'

'Perhaps I did, in a way. Rob lived fairly close to me in London, and there was always the possibility that I would keep running in to him on a day-to-day basis. It would have made things difficult if I'd stayed on and, anyway, I felt that I wanted a change from city life. It seemed natural to come back here, to my family roots.'

'Is it possible you could have a change of heart and want to go back there? When you've been that close to someone, it isn't all cut and dried, is it?'

'It is in my case. I've made my decision. I'm not going back to London.'

'Hmm.' His eyes darkened, and his mouth twisted a fraction at the corners. 'Why am I having trouble believing that?'

'Because you have a suspicious mind? Because you have absolutely no faith in me, and you're set on proving to yourself that I won't last here for longer than six months?' She shook her head. 'Think again, Alex. It isn't going to happen that way. I'm afraid you're stuck with me.'

'Maybe. But it seems to me that a lot of things have changed in your life just lately, and you might well have reacted hastily. In six months' time you might look at things in a different light.'

'I won't.' Jassie frowned, knowing that she had a lot to do to convince him of her staying power. By now, though, they had arrived back at the surgery, and in an unspoken agreement they let the matter drop as they walked into Reception together.

* * *

Over the next couple of weeks, Jassie gradually developed a working routine, where she did the home visits and morning surgeries on alternate days, and took appointments or clinics in the afternoons. It was a busy time, with a higher than average proportion of patients suffering from chest infections and viral complaints.

One lunchtime, Jassie arrived back from her home visits to find Carole talking quietly to Alex and looking concerned. Carole was a slim, dark-haired woman in her mid-thirties, with a calm and sensible way of dealing with patients. She could be relied on to sift through the calls and prioritise those that were urgent, and Jassie respected her for the way she organised the everyday running of the practice.

'Hello,' Jassie greeted her as she went to help herself to coffee. 'Is anything wrong?'

'Dr Wiseman's had to go home. We think he's suffering from some sort of virus. He looked pretty dreadful.' She grimaced. 'It means that the rotas will have to be changed until we can get a locum to fill in for him. Sorry about that, but that's the way it is, I'm afraid.'

'We'll manage,' Alex told her. 'It can't be helped.'

'What will you do if there's a lifeboat call?'

He shrugged. 'We'll deal with that if it happens. Alan might be back before too long, so there's no point in getting worked up about it. Are we all right for this afternoon?'

'I think so. Dr Hampton is taking a clinic at the hospital, and you're supposed to be doing minor operations this afternoon, so it means that we need to rely on Jassie to pull in some of Alan's afternoon appointments.'

'I can do that,' Jassie murmured.

'Are you sure?' Alex was frowning. 'I know your list is fairly full already.'

'I'll start earlier. There are always one or two patients who come in before time, and I'll have to try to be more efficient. It just means there won't be time for any chitchat…which is a pity, because it helps me to get to know the patients a little better.'

'Thanks, Jassie,' Alex said, giving her a warm smile. 'It's not often that something like this happens, but it helps if we can all pull together when it does.'

'I understand that. It's not a problem.' It was good to know that for once she was doing something right, something that might encourage him to appreciate that she could be a useful member of the team.

She turned her attention to her in-tray, which Carole had filled with a mass of papers during the morning, all needing to be dealt with on a fairly urgent basis. There would be little time to see to them once surgery started in the afternoon.

The appointments went smoothly enough, and she finally managed to catch up with herself round about teatime. She went to Reception to return a batch of patients' notes to Carole, and met up with Alex once more.

'How's it going?' he asked.

'Well enough, I think. I've only half a dozen more patients to see.'

Carole had been talking to someone on the phone, and now she said, 'All right, Mrs Stanhope, try not to worry.' She made a note on her pad. 'I don't think Dr Beaufort is available this afternoon, but I'll see if Dr Radcliffe can come out and see you as soon as possible.'

As she replaced the receiver, she looked across at Alex and said with a frown, 'Young Amy is poorly again…abdominal pain and a high temperature. Her mother sounded quite anxious on the phone. She was asking for you to go out there, but you're going to be busy doing minor ops in a few minutes, aren't you?'

Alex grimaced. 'That's right. I'm all set up to work with Sister Williams on a couple of biopsies.'

'I'm on call,' Jassie put in. 'Is there any reason I can't take this one?'

Alex turned to her. 'Of course not…it's just that I particularly wanted to keep an eye on Amy. She's a sweet little girl—six years old and chatty as they come, usually. She had chickenpox two or three weeks ago and then a few days after the rash appeared she had sickness and diarrhoea. Her temperature has been high, on and off, which seems to rule out appendicitis, with her condition settling down in between times.'

'I'll go and have a look at her as soon as I've finished dealing with my appointments.'

Alex nodded. 'Will you ring me when you've finished? I'd like to know how she is. I may not still be here by then, but you can get me on the mobile.'

'OK, I'll do that.'

The Stanhopes lived a few miles from the surgery, in a village set in a picturesque wooded valley. Jassie didn't take time out to admire the scenery, though.

This afternoon, the sky was threatening a storm, with grey cloud cover hanging low over the landscape and thunder rumbling ominously in the distance.

The child's mother, a fair haired young woman with clear blue eyes, opened the front door to Jassie and showed her into the child's bedroom.

'She's in a lot of pain, Doctor,' Julie Stanhope confided in a low voice. 'She's not been able to go to the toilet properly, to pass water, and I'm really worried about her.'

Jassie could see that the little girl was very distressed. 'Hello, Amy,' she said gently. 'I'm Dr Radcliffe. Mummy says you've not been feeling very well. Can you tell me where it hurts?'

Over the next few minutes, Jassie carefully examined the child, checking her abdomen and taking blood pressure, pulse and temperature. When she had finished, she lightly tucked the bedcovers back in place and said with a smile, 'Good girl, Amy, you've been very patient with me. You rest for a minute now, while I have a quick word with your mummy.'

Turning to Julie, she said quietly, 'She does seem to be in a good deal of pain, partly because of the urine retention, which we can relieve fairly quickly by putting in a catheter. It's possible that she has some kind of infection in her abdomen, but we need to do further tests to find out what exactly is causing the trouble...an ultrasound scan, for instance, and X-rays. I think we should admit her to the hospital so that they can do those things right away and make her more comfortable.'

Julie was pale, and clearly dismayed, but she fought

to keep her emotions under control and said, 'I'll get some of her things together, and phone her dad.'

'That's a good idea. I'll call the hospital now, and arrange for an ambulance to come and take her there.'

'Will they let me go with her in the ambulance?'

'I'm sure they will. Your presence will be reassuring for her. Perhaps you could explain things to Amy while I make the call?'

Jassie waited with them until the paramedics arrived, and then she supervised the transfer of the child to the ambulance. It was always upsetting when a young child had to go into hospital, but at least she could comfort herself with the thought that a medical team would be on the alert to deal with Amy straight away.

Glancing at her watch, she saw that it was well past six o'clock, and she guessed that Alex would be leaving the surgery about now. She would give him time to make the journey home, and ring him in a few minutes.

Going in the opposite direction to the ambulance, she started the drive to her cottage, taking a winding route along country lanes which would be quicker than the main roads. Lightning flashed overhead, and she grimaced. At least her stint on call was over for the day, and she could look forward to being home this evening.

Rounding a bend in the road, a sudden dark blur skated across her vision.

'What on earth...?'

As the image cleared she realised that a thick tree branch had sheared suddenly across her path, and was falling in a great arc to the ground.

'Oh, no...' Braking sharply to miss it, she was jerked forward in her seat, hitting her head on the windscreen before the seat belt she was wearing slammed into action and held her fast.

For some time, she sat very still, not registering much at all except for the dull pain in her head and a dazed sense of shock. There was a noise going on around her, too, an irritating bleeping which she couldn't bring herself to do anything about. By the time she realised that it must have been her mobile phone, the caller had rung off.

Oh, well. She wasn't in much of a state to talk right now, anyway. Instead, she waited until the fog in her head cleared a little, and then she slowly straightened up and undid her seat belt with shaking hands. Carefully, taking her time, she climbed out of the car and went to look at the front of her car to see what the extent of the damage was.

A large part of a tree lay on the ground, and in the semi-darkness she made out the mangled lines of the car's front bumper. The bonnet had suffered in similar fashion, crumpling under the impact of the collision.

At least she was more or less in one piece...but what if someone else came around that bend and wasn't quite so lucky? The thought spurred her into action and, with her heart beating fast now, she bent inside the car and leaned over to switch on the hazard lights. This wasn't a terribly busy road, thank heavens, but would that be warning enough?

Going back to the front of the car again, she moved around the obstruction and tugged at the wood with her bare hands, trying to ease it away and drag it back towards the ditch. Breathless from the exertion, after a while she had to admit that she wasn't getting very far.

At least she had her phone with her. Dialling the emergency services, she explained about the fallen tree and they promised to get someone out as soon as they could.

In the meantime, she tried starting her car engine. If she could back it up a little...

A motorist came around the bend and made furious use of his horn, swerving widely to avoid her car and gesturing rudely as he drove on at speed.

'Thanks a bunch,' Jassie mouthed wearily. 'Wasn't that helpful?' Still, it showed he had managed to see her in time, so that worry lessened a fraction.

A horrible grinding noise came from the engine, and she switched off the ignition, wryly acknowledging that her plan wasn't going to work. Picking up the phone again, she called her insurance company's rescue service and settled back to wait.

The mobile bleeped after a few minutes. It was probably the rescue service, calling to check where she was. She hoped that they weren't going to be delayed.

'I've been ringing you, but you weren't answering,' Alex said, sounding concerned. 'I tried to reach you at home, and then I rang your mobile. Where have you been? I expected you to call ages ago.'

She bit back a terse reply. He was worried about the child, clearly, but surely he must know that Jassie would have rung him as soon as she had been able? Or did he think that she had simply forgotten her promise?

She made an effort to stay calm and unflustered.

'I've been busy,' she told him. 'I would have called you as soon as I reached home.'

His tone was startled. 'Have you been with Amy all this time? Is something wrong? Shall I come out there?'

There was a rustling sound on the other end of the line, and she could imagine he was already hunting for his car keys, getting ready to come out and take over from her. Didn't he trust her?

'No, you don't need to do that,' she said, more sharply than she had intended. 'I'm perfectly capable of dealing with patients on my own, and if there was any need to ask for your help I would have.'

Getting that off her chest calmed her down a little, and she took time out to pull in a deep breath before adding, 'Amy's condition was deteriorating, so I decided that it needs more investigation. I've had her admitted to hospital, and I expect they're already on their way to making her feel a bit better by now. You don't need to be concerned, Alex. You can rely on me to do my job properly.'

'I wasn't suggesting that you can't.'

'Weren't you?'

The sound of a heavy vehicle trundling along the road made her turn her attention to the windscreen. It looked as though the truck that appeared on the horizon was carrying heavy lifting gear, and she breathed a sigh of relief now that at least one of her problems was about to be solved.

She turned her attention back to Alex. 'Look, I have to go now.'

'What's that I can hear?' he demanded, his senses clearly on alert. 'Are you still on the road?'

'Yes, I'm on the road.'

The driver of the truck had descended from his cab and was coming towards her. She wound her window down.

'Are you the lady who called us out?' the man asked.

'Yes, I am. You can see the problem, can't you?'

'What problem?' Alex demanded to know, but she ignored him, keeping her attention on the truck driver. He was looking around, assessing the extent of the damage. Then he turned his attention to her.

'That's a nasty bump on your head,' he said. 'Are you feeling all right?'

'I'm fine,' she murmured, trying a weary smile.

'What's going on?' Alex interrupted tersely.

'Nothing,' she said tautly. His questioning was beginning to make her head throb. 'Look, I really have to go now. I'll talk to you later.'

She cut the call and switched off the phone so that he couldn't disturb her any more.

'We'll put some warning lamps up,' the man said. 'Keep people from getting into trouble.'

He busied himself with that for a while, then came to inspect the part of the tree that had fallen to the ground.

'Could have been diseased, I suppose,' he said. 'Wouldn't help much, with all this lightning about. I'll have it moved out of the way in a jiff.'

'That's good.'

The whole operation took about twenty minutes, and when he had finished the man asked, 'That car of yours not working? The front end looks pretty well bashed in.'

She shook her head. 'Someone's on his way to help.'

'He'll need a tow truck from the looks of things. Will you be all right if I go off and leave you, or do you want me to wait with you?'

'I'll be OK. You don't need to wait, but thanks for the offer.'

He took a final look around. 'Keep the warning lights in place until your car's moved out of the way. Then you can put them at the side of the road and I'll pick them up in the morning.'

He left her to it, and she sank back in her seat, resting her aching head against the upholstered support and closing her eyes. How much longer would she have to wait for the rescue service to come along? A good half an hour must have gone by already.

A tap on the window some five minutes later brought her upright again. She blinked into the darkness and was shocked to see Alex standing there.

For the second time that evening, she wound the window down.

'I had the feeling something was wrong,' he said curtly. 'What's going on? Why didn't you tell me you had been in an accident?'

Jassie sighed inwardly. Why couldn't the rescue service have reached her first? She was never going to prove herself to be capable and in control of things at this rate, and the last thing she needed was to give him more ammunition to fire at her.

CHAPTER FOUR

JASSIE'S defences went on urgent standby. 'Who said that I was in any trouble? Everything's perfectly under control.'

'It's fairly obvious to me that it isn't, by any stretch of the imagination,' Alex argued disagreeably. 'Your car's a wreck, you're stranded out here miles from anywhere and there's a nasty gash on your head that needs attention. If you seriously believe that constitutes everything being fine and dandy, I think we need to thoroughly reassess your mental state.'

'That would be altogether too dramatic, don't you think?' She was in no mood for a tussle with him right now. 'What I meant was that the rescue service is on its way.'

She frowned. 'What are you doing here, anyway? How did you find me?'

'I added two and two together and guessed that you would have come home across country. Then it was just a question of tracing the route you must have taken.'

'I can't think why you would want to do that.'

'Isn't it obvious? After hearing you talking to that man on the phone, I knew I needed to come and find out what had happened. I had visions of you being stranded out here on a dark country lane in goodness knows what condition.'

He didn't sound too pleased about having to come after her, and who could blame him for that? He had been forced to abandon his plans for the evening and come after her, and she doubted whether that would endear her to him. It wasn't that he felt any great concern for her, of course...he was probably worried that, with Alan out of action, the practice couldn't afford to have another doctor off sick.

'It was thoughtful of you to come and find me,' she said huskily. 'But you can see that I'm perfectly safe—I just took a bit of a knock, that's all.'

'What happened?' he asked.

'A tree came down and I had to brake suddenly to avoid crashing into it.'

'From the state of your car it doesn't look as though you succeeded too well,' he said, a cool glint coming into his eyes. 'Though I'm more concerned about the bang to your head. Weren't you wearing a seat belt?'

'Of course I was.' Jassie shrugged lightly, then winced as she felt a degree of tenderness around her neck and shoulders. 'The damage could have been much worse otherwise.'

He frowned. 'Perhaps you ought to have had your seat belt checked or, better still, maybe you should change the car for a younger model. The brakes don't seem too good, and you said before that the heater wasn't working. How many other things aren't up to scratch? Don't you think, as a doctor, you ought to drive around in something more reliable than this old thing?'

'I'm really not in the mood for a lecture,' she murmured crossly, unnerved by the tension in his manner.

'My car is...was...perfectly roadworthy, and if you can't do anything other than have a go at me, I'd really prefer it if you went back home.'

He grimaced. 'I'm sure you would. I don't intend to oblige you, though. It isn't every day I come across a colleague stranded on a country lane.'

Alex looked at her thoughtfully. 'Perhaps you'd better come and sit in my car, and let me see what damage you've done to yourself.'

'I can see to it myself later.' She flapped a hand at him and moved jerkily, a mistake clearly because a feeling of nausea suddenly swept over her. She sucked in a deep breath and swallowed hard as beads of perspiration began to break out on her brow.

'Are you going to be sick?'

She fervently hoped not. She shook her head, not wanting to speak, and he said on a decisive note, 'Look, as soon as you feel up to it, I'm going to get you out of here. My medical bag's in the car, and I can at least dress the wound for you. Besides, you'll have to get out of here when the rescue service arrives to move the car.'

The feverishness she had experienced died away, and in its place she began to feel shivery. It was probably reaction setting in, and she huddled into herself, shutting out the world for a moment or two, until Alex began to ease her out of her seat. All at once it was easier to give in than to try to make a stand and she didn't put up any resistance as he put an arm around her and helped her towards his car.

Jassie sat back in the warmth of his passenger seat, enjoying the luxurious feel of the leather upholstery and the soothing touch of his fingers as he cleaned the cut on her brow and covered it with a dressing.

Perhaps tomorrow she could work on being independent, when she was feeling a bit stronger.

'It'll be sore, and you'll probably have a throbbing headache for a while, but at least I can keep you warm and comfortable for now,' he said quietly. 'I'll get the travel rug from the boot.'

He got out of the car and went to retrieve the rug, and it was as though a draught of cold air suddenly swirled around her. She hadn't been aware of how much she had appreciated his warm, reassuring presence until he'd left her, and now she waited anxiously for his return.

Within a moment or two, he was back. 'Here you are. This should help.'

He looked at her in the shadowy interior of the car, and frowned. 'You're very pale. I don't want you going into shock.'

'I'll be all right,' she said huskily. 'It's just that it all seems to be catching up with me now.'

He carefully wrapped the rug around her, and she absorbed the comfort of it and sank back into the seat, thankful for the chance to rest again and not have to think.

When the rescue service arrived, just a minute or so later, she made a move to get out of the car, but Alex gently pushed her back in the seat.

'I'll deal with it,' he said. At the back of her mind, she knew she should be sorting it out herself, but every movement made her head throb and for the moment she was glad that he had taken charge.

'He's going to tow it to the local garage,' Alex told her when he came back, 'and the insurance company will arrange for a hire car to be sent to your house early tomorrow.'

'Good,' she murmured. 'At least that's settled.'

He drove her home and insisted on seeing her into the cottage.

'Go and sit down and keep the blanket round you,' he ordered when she would have gone to fill the kettle at the sink. 'I'll put the kettle on and fix you a hot drink so that you can take your headache tablets.'

She opened her mouth to say something and he turned her around and marched her out of the kitchen.

'Not another word,' he said. 'Go and put your feet up on the settee.' As an afterthought, he tacked on, 'I don't suppose you've eaten yet, have you?'

She shook her head. 'I'm not sure that I want anything.'

'You may do later,' he said laconically. 'Do you like pizza?' When she nodded, he smiled. 'Good. Mushrooms? Ham?' And when she didn't disagree, he took out his mobile and started to dial. 'I'll order a big one with extra toppings. I'm famished.'

While they were waiting for the delivery, he brought her a cup of tea and a couple of paracetamol, and after a while she began to feel better. She pushed the blanket to one side.

'Are you warmer now?'

'Lovely and warm, thanks.'

'That's good,' he murmured. 'Now all you need to do is get some food inside you, and you might be on top of things again.'

Jassie gave him a small grin. 'I haven't been this cosseted since my brother tipped me out of a tree.'

His brow lifted. 'Did he do that on purpose?'

She laughed. 'Oh, no. It was purely accidental, and it was probably my own fault. I used to tag along with Nick and Steve whenever I had the chance, and even when they didn't want me around I'd do my best to keep up with them.'

He gave a wry smile. 'I can imagine. So you followed them up a tree and found yourself pushed out?'

'I wasn't pushed.' She pulled a face, remembering. 'It was actually the first time that I'd ever climbed one. I wanted a piece of the action, and Steve headed for the top branches of an old oak. He didn't realise I was behind him, and when he turned around suddenly he knocked me off my perch. I was OK, just wounded pride really, but they were worried sick in case I'd got a brain injury or something.'

'I don't suppose it put you off trying again?'

She shook her head. 'Not at all. I was back up there the first chance I got.'

'Somehow that doesn't surprise me.'

The pizza arrived as he finished speaking and he went to collect it, coming back into the room with a large carton.

'Try some of this,' he said, handing her a section of the pizza. She bit into it, suddenly realising how hungry she was and enjoying the texture and the taste of melted cheese, red peppers and mushrooms.

'Mmm…this is wonderful,' she said.

'It is.' He came to sit beside her on the settee, looking at her quizzically. 'You were telling me about your brothers. Did you try to keep up with them in everything?'

'Most of the time. I didn't want them to be able to do anything that I couldn't do. I wasn't going to let them run rings around me. They thought I was a pain, I suppose, but if anybody caused me any trouble they would have defended me to the last. I was their little sister, and they were very protective.'

'It sounds as though you were very close.'

'We were…we are…'

Alex frowned. 'Yet you said things had been awkward between you and your brother Nick lately. Do you want to tell me what happened?'

She wasn't sure how much of it she could explain, but she said, 'There was a problem at the place where he worked. He was involved in a research programme, and he felt that some changes could have been made to make the working environment better and to allow his team to work more efficiently. He approached Rob with his ideas, but Rob wasn't keen on making any changes. He said they weren't cost-efficient.'

Jassie hesitated, thinking about the way things had gone downhill after that. 'It caused a lot of bad feeling, and in the end Nick resigned. I was caught between the two of them. My loyalties were split. I understood why Nick wanted things altered, and I could sympathise with him, but at the same time I needed to listen to Rob's side of things.'

Frowning, she went on, 'I think Nick felt that because Rob and I were engaged, he had caused a problem between us, and it made it difficult for me to talk to him about what was going on. He was always on the defensive, and didn't give me a chance to tell him that I didn't blame him for anything.'

'And you were hoping that you might get the chance to talk to him properly while he's down here on holiday?'

'Yes. It would be nice to be able to smooth things over. My family is important to me.'

'I can understand how you feel. I wouldn't like any bad feeling between myself and my parents or my brother.'

'Do they live locally?'

'My parents do. My brother's abroad at the moment, working for the Red Cross.'

'I've always wondered what it would be like to do that. I'm not sure I'd want to be based too far away from the UK, though. I think I need to be fairly close to my roots.'

'It's different for women, I imagine, especially if you're thinking of getting married at some point and raising a family.'

'Yes, there is that.' She was quiet for a moment, contemplating what might have been if things with Rob hadn't turned out the way they had. But that was all over now, and she pushed the thought to one side, looking up to find Alex studying her thoughtfully.

On a lighter note, she said, 'Do you hear from your brother very often?'

'He writes fairly regularly, and we get phone calls in between, so my parents don't feel that they're too cut off from him. Of course, my mother always thinks he's not getting enough to eat, but that's mothers all over, isn't it?'

Jassie smiled, and stretched lazily. 'If they could see us now... I think I've eaten too much...'

'At least your colour's better than it was earlier. You were so pale...I was afraid you might be suffering from concussion.'

'I *was* feeling irritable. I just wanted you to go away and leave me alone...but now I think it's fortunate you refused.' She smiled up at him, relieved that he was by her side.

'So am I.' He looked at her searchingly, and murmured, 'I'm glad you're all right.'

'I'm sorry if I caused you any worry, but I'm fine now, really.' Her cheeks dimpled and she added softly, 'You've been very good, looking after me like this.'

His glance moved over her, and he murmured lightly, 'It was my pleasure.' Then, almost on an impulse it seemed, he bent his head towards her and kissed her gently on the mouth.

It was so unexpected that a flare of heat ran through her entire body and her lips quivered, yearning for more. She leaned towards him, her body trembling, and she touched his arm, her fingers trailing lightly over the toughened sinews, more to reassure herself that he was truly there, that this was really happening.

His gaze tangled with hers, and for an aching moment she thought that he was going to kiss her again. But then he gave a ragged sigh, and shook his head as though to clear it.

She stared at him, her heart pounding, her emotions on a roller-coaster ride as he got fluidly to his feet and moved away from her.

'Try and get some rest,' he said in a roughened

voice. 'It's late, and we both have to work in the morning.' He reached for his jacket, which he had dropped casually over the back of a chair. 'I'll see you tomorrow. Give me a ring if your hire car doesn't turn up and I'll give you a lift in to work—or let me know if you feel unwell again.'

'I will,' she said huskily, feeling close to tears all at once and not knowing why.

As things turned out, she didn't need to call him. A hire car was waiting for her first thing next morning, as promised, and a week later her own car was back from the garage, looking as though nothing untoward had happened.

She tried to push the events of that day out of her mind. It was madness to even contemplate getting involved with Alex and, anyway, after what had happened between her and Rob, she wasn't at all sure that she could trust her instincts any more.

Instead, she made up her mind to concentrate totally on her job, and thankfully Alex appeared to be doing the same. They were busy, with Alan still off work with an unexplained virus, and only patchy locum cover.

At the surgery, around lunchtime one day, when her last patient of the morning walked into her room, she was surprised to see someone she recognised. It was the young woman she had met at the Harbour Inn, and her little boy, Sam, was with her, taking a curious look around the room.

'Sarah, hello,' Jassie said, looking up at her in surprise. 'And Sam, too. I didn't expect to see either of you here. Do you live locally?'

'We live in a village just a couple of miles from here,' Sarah answered, returning her smile.

'I should have realised. Alex said he was your doctor.'

Sarah chuckled. 'I'm not surprised you didn't know. He came out on the lifeboat that day, otherwise we wouldn't have been in the same place at the same time. We were both some way from home.'

'And your brother...how is he? He punctured his lung, if I remember rightly.'

'He's on the mend, I think. He's home from the hospital, anyway—bruised and sore, but getting better every day.'

'That's good news, isn't it?'

Sarah returned her smile. 'Yes, it is.'

'And how are you? Is your wrist still giving you trouble?'

'Oh, no, I'm fine.' She glanced down at the little boy who was wriggling on her lap, trying to reach the pot of pens on Jassie's desk. 'No, Sam, you can't have those,' she murmured, then to Jassie she said, 'It's Sam, here, who's in the wars.'

'Oh, poor little chap. What seems to be the problem?'

'He's very fretful just lately. He keeps pulling at his ear, and when I looked to see what was wrong it looked a bit inflamed. I feel awful because I'd put his irritability down to disturbed nights after we'd been on the yacht that day. I thought perhaps he was having nightmares about it. I hate to think that he's been in pain all the time and I didn't know about it.'

'It happens that way sometimes. I'll have a look at him, if you can manage to keep him on your lap for a while.'

She smiled at Sam, who looked as though he might be feverish, with patches of bright colour on his cheeks.

'Hello, young man,' she said softly. 'Do you remember me? I'm Jassie.' He nodded sombrely and she added quietly, 'Are you feeling poorly? Can you tell me where it hurts?'

It was always difficult, dealing with very young children, but Jassie had found that as long as she gave them time to get used to her, they usually responded to a gentle, reassuring manner.

Sam looked warily at her, but mumbled, 'Hurt.' He tugged at his ear.

'Your ear hurts, does it? Oh, dear, you poor little man. Perhaps I could have a look at it?' He wasn't at all keen on that suggestion, so she searched in a drawer and brought out a soft little tiger from a jumble of toys that she kept specially for children who might be unwilling to co-operate. 'Tell you what,' she murmured coaxingly, 'you play with him for a minute while I have a quick look.'

Sam was intrigued by the little animal. 'Raargh!' he said, his eyes widening, and Jassie laughed.

'That's right,' she agreed cheerfully. 'He's very fierce, isn't he? Raargh!'

Sam chuckled, and while he was occupied with playing stalking tiger games along the arm of his mother's chair, she made a quick examination, asking Sarah, 'Has he been unwell at all lately?'

'He's had a bit of a cough and a cold for the last few weeks and, as I said, he's been restless the last couple of nights.'

Jassie nodded. 'He's a bit feverish, and there's a discharge coming from the ear, which really needs to be treated with an antibiotic medicine. I can let you have a prescription for that. You could give him Calpol for the pain, and that will help bring his temperature down as well.'

'Thank you. I'm so relieved, now that I've brought him to you. They can't tell you what's wrong when they're so little, can they? And I hate to think that he's hurting.'

'Ear infections can be horrible, can't they? But I'm sure he'll be all right in a few days.' She wrote out the prescription and handed it to Sarah. 'It was good to see you again,' she said as her patient got up to leave.

'You, too. Perhaps we'll meet again some time...hopefully when there's nothing wrong with either me or Sam.' Sarah laughed. 'We'll keep in touch, anyway.'

Jassie smiled. 'I'd like that.'

With lunch next on her agenda, Jassie tidied up her desk and went into Reception to pass the packages of patients' notes to Carole for filing. Alex was already there, taking a phone call and looking concerned.

'Do you know how many people are injured?' he was saying. 'Yes, that's a good idea—the helicopter can only take so many. No, Dr Wiseman is ill, I'm afraid, and Dr Hampton isn't expected until afternoon surgery. I'll get over to you right away. I should be with you in ten minutes.'

As he put down the phone, he was already reaching for his medical bag and calling to Carole for extra supplies.

'What's happened?' Jassie asked.

'There's a cargo ship in trouble. It was blown off course in a gale and went too close to rocks. It's caused a breach in the hold, and the cargo is shifting. As far as I know, about half a dozen of the crewmen have been injured. Mostly fractures, from the sound of it, but no fatalities thankfully. The lifeboat's going out to help pick up the rest of the crew.'

'I'll come with you,' Jassie said.

'No. It's too dangerous for you to go along. The ship's likely to sink before too long.'

'You need me,' she insisted. 'Whoever you were speaking to was asking for Dr Wiseman to go as well, wasn't he?'

'It makes no difference. You're needed here.'

'Dr Hampton will deal with any problems here.' She was already shrugging into her jacket and starting to collect together drugs and syringes, checking off a list in her head.

'The lifeboat's no place for a woman. The first breath of a gale and you'd be knocked for six.'

Within minutes he was on his way out of the surgery and heading towards his car, and she hurried to keep up with him.

'Don't be so sexist. You knew I was a woman when I applied for the job.'

'Maybe. But I wasn't expecting someone like you.'
'Meaning?'

He opened his car door and slid into the driver's seat. 'Meaning I shall be far too busy attending to the injured to have time to nursemaid you as well.'

'And I'll be too busy myself for you to have the chance,' she said through gritted teeth, wrenching open the passenger door and getting in beside him.

'I don't have time to argue with you,' he muttered tersely. 'I don't want you coming along.'

'Too bad,' she threw back, fastening her seat belt. 'You've got me.' He could hardly throw her out, and she wouldn't give him the chance to simply leave her behind.

He said something under his breath that she found hard to decipher, but the words 'stubborn' and 'headstrong' surfaced as he started the car and slammed the car into gear. Then he hit the accelerator and turned the car onto the coast road.

His ill-temper wasn't going to change anything. She'd made up her mind, and no amount of chauvinist prejudice was going to throw her off course. She'd honed her fighting spirit in umpteen arguments with her brothers, and she'd come out on the winning side enough times to show her that she could topple his house of cards easily enough.

The lifeboat station was on a plateau, bounded by granite cliffs to the rear and a long sweep of beach at either side. The lifeboat was ready to launch from the slipway, and Jassie hurried aboard, ignored by Alex who had gone to speak to the skipper. One of the crewmen offered her a helping hand.

'Hello. I'm Simon,' he said. 'Let me fix you up with a weatherproof coat and life-jacket.' He gave her a searching look. 'I think we've met before, briefly.'

'Have we?' He was a young man, around thirty years of age, and as she searched her memory she said thoughtfully, 'I think you might have been at the Harbour Inn at the same time as me a while back.' She smiled her thanks as he handed her a life-jacket, and then she concentrated on buckling the straps in place. 'I'm Dr Radcliffe,' she told him. 'Jassie.'

'Glad to have you aboard, Jassie. Have you done much sailing?' Simon asked, and when she shook her head, he added, 'So is this your first stint as a doctor on board the lifeboat?'

'That's right.'

'You'll be OK,' he said confidently. 'There's a westerly gale blowing, though, so things could get fierce once we're out at sea. Hold on tight and stay near the rail if you start to feel a bit queasy.'

'I'll do that,' she told him, and hoped that she wouldn't disgrace herself by succumbing to that particular weakness.

Alex took the gale in his stride. He looked tough and confident and very capable, and it was the thought that he would be on the lookout for any sign of frailty in her that kept her mind sharp and her determination keen.

When they reached the cargo ship, there was no time to think about hostilities. They climbed aboard and the lifeboat chief took them to where the most seriously injured men were lying belowdeck, all needing immediate attention. Conditions were precarious down there, with the ship being tossed by heavy seas and the danger of shifting cargo ever present, and it was a struggle to simply keep her balance.

Between them, she and Alex made a quick assessment of their patients' conditions.

'This one's in a bad way,' Alex muttered, bending down beside a man who had suffered a nasty head injury. He was unconscious and Jassie guessed he would need surgery fairly soon if he was to have any chance at all. Alex checked his airway, and then set about intubating him, hooking him up to an oxygen supply.

As soon as Jassie saw that Alex could manage alone, she left him to it, turning her attention to supporting vital signs in the others. She soon found herself working on sheer instinct, thankful for all her professional training.

One man's pulse was faltering, and she struggled to establish a steady rhythm before moving on to other patients, splinting broken limbs and injecting painkillers, trying to keep from stumbling as she moved from one man to another, while all the time the ship lurched and dipped on the heaving sea.

One of the men was barely conscious, trapped beneath a collapsed pillar of wood. While his fellow crewmen worked to move the weight that was crushing his chest, she worked quickly to fix an intravenous drip in place. She tried to ignore the ominous creaking of timbers and the sounds of disintegration going on all around her.

'Look out,' Alex shouted suddenly, and as she glanced behind her, she saw him get to his feet. His patient was being transferred to a makeshift stretcher. 'Get out of the way.' He signalled to her to move, and in the next moment she saw a huge crate bearing slowly down on her, sliding across the floor of the hold as the ship listed to one side.

There was no way she could get out of the way without deserting her patient, and the thought of leaving him lying there utterly defenceless filled her with horror. Instinctively, she bent over him in a protective arch, and waited for the crunch.

It didn't come. As the seconds stretched without any disaster happening, she gradually allowed herself to breathe again and slowly turned to see what had happened.

Alex and several of the able-bodied crewmen had blocked the path of the crate and were pitting their strength against it, making an effort to wedge it against a safety barrier.

'Get out of there,' Alex said urgently. 'We might not be able to hold it like this for much longer.'

'I can't,' she said, shaking her head. 'I must stay with him. I need to get this tube in place. As soon as the timber is lifted away from him, we can perhaps pull him to safety.'

Someone came to take Alex's place, and he quickly moved to her side, anchoring his body between her and the immediate danger. The ship lurched again, its hulk protesting under the strain, and Jassie hurried to stabilise the man's condition.

'I think he's bleeding internally,' she whispered. The man looked ashen, and was fading in and out of consciousness, perhaps mercifully so in the circumstances. 'We need to get him to surgery fast.'

Alex nodded, twisting around to face the men who were working on the timber. 'How's it going? Are you about ready to lift?'

'It's trapped at one end. Give us another couple of minutes.'

'OK.' He turned back to Jassie. 'As soon as they're ready, we'll slide him out of the way. What have you given him?'

'Morphine. That should hold him till we get him to hospital.'

They heard the drone of a helicopter overhead, but Alex stayed by her side.

'We're ready to lift now,' a crewman said.

'OK,' Alex said. 'After a count of three, we'll slide him out. Here goes. One...two...three...now!'

'Careful, easy does it.' Jassie moved as one with Alex until they had pulled their patient clear. 'All right, that's it, let's get him transferred to the stretcher quickly.'

'There's nothing more we can do for him here,' Alex said crisply after a minute or two. 'The medical team in the helicopter will take over now. The man with head injuries and the one with the broken leg need to go with him. Jassie, I want you out of here now. Go up on deck with Simon and help organise the transfer.'

A second helicopter arrived a few minutes later to take off the other crew members who were not so seriously injured, and Alex came up from the hold to help supervise their move.

Watching from the deck, Jassie felt relief flood through her as the Sea King helicopter started the return journey towards the coast. The sooner the injured reached hospital, the better their chances of making a good recovery.

She watched the helicopter disappear into the distance, and clung to the rail as the ship bucked and heaved on the raging water. Was it listing more than it had been earlier, or was her mind playing tricks on her? No...as her body swayed to counteract the tilt of the deck beneath her, she knew that it wasn't her imagination.

Feeling the colour drain from her face, she turned to see Alex making his way towards her.

'Are we sinking already?' she asked fearfully, raising her voice to counteract the roar of the wind and the ill-humoured lashing of the sea.

'Maybe...but it'll take a while yet,' Alex answered. 'They'll get us back on board the lifeboat before that happens. They're still taking the rest of the crew off.' He frowned, dashing the salt spray from his face with the back of his hand. 'Are you all right?'

She wasn't all right. Far from it. In fact, now that the ordeal of tending to their patients was over she was beginning to feel unbelievably shaky, and the full horror of their situation was gradually dawning on her. They were out in a force-ten gale, lashed by waves that were higher than she had ever seen, on a ship that was slowly taking on water. She was being thrown this way and that so furiously that she had to hold on to the rail simply to keep from toppling overboard.

She gritted her teeth. 'Yes, I'm OK.' She wasn't

going to admit any of her anxieties to Alex. Instead, she forced herself to get a grip and overcome the shakiness, breathing deeply to counteract the wave of nausea that threatened to overwhelm her.

Still frowning, Alex moved closer, putting an arm around her and holding her tight. 'Don't worry, I've got you.'

The ship lurched again, and she would have been thrown sideways if it hadn't been for him steadying her and lending support. Recovering her balance, she fought to keep from retching.

'Simon and the chief are coming over,' he said, looking out to sea, where an inflatable craft was edging alongside. 'They must be ready to take us back to the lifeboat. Keep close to me and I'll help you to keep your footing.'

Alex's strength gave Jassie the courage to go on. He wasn't letting go of her, and she made a supreme effort to overcome her fear of being lost overboard. She felt oddly secure, now that Alex was by her side.

Once they were safely back on board the lifeboat, Jassie's stomach stopped churning at last, and she began to feel foolish for getting into such a state. How could she have been so afraid when all around her people were injured and suffering far worse than she was?

She looked around, and saw that the skipper was beckoning to Alex.

'I think the chief wants a word with you,' she said.

'I'll go and talk to him in a moment.' He studied her face keenly. 'Are you going to be OK? You look deathly white.'

She nodded. 'I'm fine now. Thanks for being there with me, Alex. I'm sorry for making such a fool of myself.'

'You didn't. Anyone would have been scared out there. Even seasoned sailors have a healthy respect for the sea and what it can do at its worst. You shouldn't blame yourself for recognising that.'

Simon came to join them. 'I'll look after Jassie while you go and talk to the skipper,' he said. 'I think he wants you to take a look at his hand. He gashed it a while back. I don't think it's too bad, but it might need a stitch or two. Jassie will be OK with me.'

Still looking doubtful, Alex said, 'Will you take her into the cabin so that she can get warmed up a bit? Give her something hot to drink?'

'Sure thing. Come on, Jassie.' Simon led her away towards the cabin, but all the time she was conscious of Alex's gaze on her.

'I've some soup in a flask,' Simon told her. 'That'll warm you up.'

He handed her a mug, and she sipped gratefully, cheered by the hot liquid, feeling the warmth slowly seep into her bones.

'It's a wild one out there, but at least you're still in one piece,' he said with a grin.

'Just about.' She could laugh with him now that she was safely back on board the lifeboat and in the shelter of the well-lit cabin. 'You must be dedicated to keep on doing this kind of work, year after year,' she said with a rueful grimace. 'How often do you get called out?'

'I'm on call roughly once a month. Other times I'm

land based, showing people around the boat and the lifeboat station. They seem to like it.'

'Well, you do a marvellous job. Do you get many people wanting to look around?'

He nodded. 'A lot in the tourist season, especially children. My own boy, Daniel, loves to come on board and try his hand at the wheel and explore. People are funny, you know. They always think the boat's somehow romantic and inspiring—even when they've looked round it and seen how cramped the quarters are, they think it's great. I could tell them the reality isn't nearly so fairy-tale as they imagine.'

Jassie laughed with him, and when she heard the sound of the cabin door opening, she looked up to see Alex come in.

'You seem to have recovered well enough,' he said, his gaze going from one to the other and then shifting back to narrow on her flushed cheeks. 'Up on deck, I thought you looked about ready to faint.'

'It was probably just the cold that got to me,' she murmured. 'I'm feeling much better now. Simon's given me some soup, and that helped a lot.'

'I'm sure it did.' Alex's features were shuttered now, and she had no way of knowing what he was thinking. 'If you don't need me, then,' he said, 'I'll go back up on deck. I just came to say that the storm's settling down and we'll be able to head straight back to the station.' He turned away and left the cabin.

Simon frowned, saying on a low note, 'He's quieter than usual. I wonder what's eating him.'

Jassie was thoughtful for a moment. Was Alex still annoyed with her for insisting on coming along? Now that things had calmed down, he might have had time to assess everything that had happened.

She finished off the last of her soup. 'I expect he's concerned about some of the injured who are being taken to hospital. The only consolation we have is that a team will be waiting for them, ready to operate as soon as they arrive.'

'You both did very well. Especially you, considering it was your first time on this sort of mission.'

She smiled. 'Thanks for that, Simon.' He was bolstering her confidence, and knowing that she had done a good job as far as her patients were concerned made her feel a little happier.

She went back up on deck and a few minutes later she and Alex disembarked at the lifeboat station. They said their goodbyes to the crew and walked to Alex's car which was parked nearby.

Alex unlocked it without saying anything, opening the passenger door for her to get in. His silence unnerved her. There was a brooding quality to his manner, and she cast a surreptitious glance his way as he slid into the driver's seat beside her. She didn't know what to make of his mood.

'You're very quiet,' she said, as he started the car and turned the wheel towards the coast road. 'Are you worried about the injured men?'

He shook his head. 'We did what we could for them. It's up to the surgeons to pull them through now.'

'If it isn't that, what is it? I know something's wrong.'

'I said before, Jassie, I don't feel comfortable having you work on the lifeboats. You did well back there, you did an excellent job, but you shouldn't have been in that position in the first place. Your life was in danger, and it doesn't feel right to me that you should put yourself at such risk.'

'Aren't you taking the same sort of risks every time you go out with the lifeboat?'

His eyes narrowed. 'That isn't the point. As one of the senior partners I'm responsible for the people in my team.'

'I don't believe that you're responsible for me in any way,' she insisted, 'and I wouldn't have accepted this job if I hadn't felt that I could do it. Nothing has happened since then to change my mind. In fact, if I'm absolutely honest, now that it's over, I can look back on it and think that I've been on my very first lifeboat mission, and it was scary, yes, but in a way it was exhilarating, too.'

'I'm glad you think so,' he muttered. He drew up outside her cottage and cut the engine.

She asked quietly, 'Would you like to come in for a coffee?'

He shook his head. 'I'd better not. I have to go back to the surgery and relieve Dr Hampton. He has a meeting later on, and if I go now he might just make it on time.'

She had to fight the feeling of disappointment that swept over her, but she said lightly, 'All right, then. I'll see you tomorrow.'

He nodded, turning the key in the ignition again, and the engine throbbed into life.

She watched him drive away, and wondered how it

was that she should suddenly feel so bereft and alone. She ought to be feeling uplifted because this afternoon, surely, she had proved that she was every bit as capable of doing the job as a man.

The plain truth was, though, that no matter how hard she worked to do a professional job, Alex was still convinced that she didn't belong here, and right now it was more important to her than ever that he accepted she wasn't just along for the ride.

CHAPTER FIVE

JASSIE woke the next day to find the sun streaming in through her window and the birds in full song outside. She blinked, rubbing the sleep from her eyes and scrabbled for her watch, trying to focus on an analogue display that didn't make any sense at all. That couldn't possibly be the right time...could it? She was going to be late for work unless she got a move on.

There was no time for breakfast this morning, so she made do with just a quick cup of coffee before she dashed out of the house and set off to drive to the health centre.

'Oh, there you are,' Carole greeted her as she hurried into Reception a few minutes later. 'You're usually here bright and early. Have you been having some problems this morning?'

'I must have slept through the alarm,' Jassie said, a little out of breath through rushing. It was probably the aftermath of the adrenaline surge yesterday that had caused her to sleep so deeply. She shrugged out of her jacket and put it on a hanger in the cloakroom.

'Well, you're here now, that's the main thing. Alex was about to send out a search party.'

Jassie winced. She'd hoped he wouldn't have noticed. 'I don't see him around. Is he taking surgery already?'

Carole nodded. 'He made an early start because he

wants to go and see Dr Wiseman as soon as he can this morning. He rang him to see how he was doing, and I don't think he sounded too good.'

'Oh? Did Alex say what's wrong with him?'

'He was struggling to get his breath apparently, and didn't have the strength to get out of bed. This virus seems to be really dragging him down. It isn't like Alan to give in, you know. He's usually always on the go, trying to keep on top of things.'

'Yes, I had that impression of him,' Jassie admitted. 'I haven't seen much of him since I started here, but he struck me as being someone who was ultra-efficient and always busy. I wouldn't mind going along with Alex to see him. It sounds as though he could do with cheering up a bit, and we might be able to do something to make him more comfortable.'

'I'll mention it to Alex when I see him.' Carole glanced down at her notepad. 'In the meantime, I've taken some messages for you and put them in your tray so that you can deal with them later—there was nothing urgent—and I've organised your post for you. Would you like me to bring you a cup of coffee in about ten minutes, after you've had a chance to get yourself sorted?'

'Thanks, Carole. You're a treasure. I'll go and make a start right away.'

Hurrying to her room, she switched on the computer, scanned her list and pressed the buzzer, ready for the first patient.

She worked continuously, not even stopping for a break mid-morning, and managed to catch up with things round about lunchtime. There was a stack of post still to be dealt with, though, and she had made a start on that when Alex came into Reception.

'You've finished seeing your patients, then?'

Looking up from the hospital report she was reading she nodded briefly. 'A few minutes ago, yes. I was hoping to clear my desk so that I could go with you to see Alan. Would you mind if I tag along?'

'Of course not. Carole mentioned that you wanted to come with me. Actually, I think it's a good idea. Alan's too stoical for his own good, and I've a feeling that he needs help more than he's letting on. With both of us to contend with, he might relent and see sense.'

'That's true.' She glanced down at the hospital report once more, and then passed it to him. 'This is about Amy...do you remember, the little girl with the abdominal pain and fever? She's being treated for a pelvic appendix abscess...they've drained it, and they're treating the infection with antibiotics.'

He made a face. 'Poor child. She must have been in a lot of pain. It's a good thing that you acted as quickly as you did, or she might have been in an even worse condition.'

'I guessed it might be something along those lines that was causing her illness. As it is, though, she seems to be doing all right now. In fact, she'll probably be home soon—if she hasn't been released from hospital already.'

Alex nodded, handing the report back to her. 'She's a plucky little girl. I'm glad her illness was caught in time.' He watched her put the paper into a tray, ready for filing. 'If you're all finished here, we'll go and see Alan.'

'Yes, I'm ready now.' Jassie shrugged on her jacket and went out with him to his car. Her stomach was beginning to complain about the lack of breakfast, but she guessed she would have to wait awhile longer before she could grab herself some lunch.

Alan lived about four miles from the surgery, in a quiet cul-de-sac made up of detached houses and neatly kept lawns. Alex rang the doorbell and they waited for a minute or two, but when there was no answer Alex said quietly, 'We'd better try around the back.'

They let themselves in through the back door, calling out to Alan a few times, but there was still no answer.

'He must be in bed,' Jassie said. 'Let's go and take a look upstairs.'

Alan was in the main bedroom, huddled under a duvet and looking ghastly. There was a film of sweat on his brow, his black hair was unkempt and his eyes were dull. They could hear the harsh rasp of his breath as he tried to pull air into his lungs.

'Alan, you should have let us know you were feeling this low,' Jassie said, going over to him and looking at him in concern. He was in his late thirties, usually strong and vital, but he had clearly lost weight and looked thin and haggard now. 'Why didn't you tell us what was happening to you?'

'You have enough to do, without taking time out to fuss over me,' he said, his breathing coming in sharp bursts in between the words. 'I feel bad enough as it is, about letting you down.'

'You're not letting us down,' Alex told him firmly.

'We've a locum helping out, and you have no need to feel anxious about the practice. We're doing fine. What's important is that you get better.' He opened up his medical bag. 'I want to examine you, and see what's going on. Is it all right if I do that?'

Alan nodded, probably beyond caring too much what was said or done, and Alex took time to carefully listen to his chest through the stethoscope, and then take his temperature. After a while he shook his head and said gently, 'From the looks of things, you have pneumonia. I think you'd be better off in hospital, where you can be cared for properly.'

Alan tried to protest, but it was fairly obvious that he hadn't the strength to argue, and in the end he gave in and allowed them to ferry him to the hospital. Jassie quickly packed a few things for him, and within less than an hour he had been admitted to a ward and was being given oxygen and antibiotics. They saw him settled in, but left after a while when it was clear he needed to get some rest.

'Doesn't he have any family?' Jassie asked.

'I think his parents and his sister live about ten miles away, so it won't be too difficult for them to come over and visit. He doesn't seem to have told them he was ill, or they would have come to stay with him, I'm sure. He recently separated from his wife, so I think perhaps we had better contact her as well and let her know what's happening. I expect he's been neglecting himself since she left, and that's maybe why things got out of hand.'

Jassie's mobile rang just then, as they were heading for the main doors, and Alex said, 'While you're taking that, I'll go and phone Alan's relatives. I'll meet you outside in a little while.'

'OK.' She went and sat outside on a bench and took the call.

Rob's voice startled her, coming firm and clear out of the blue. 'Hello, Jassie. How are you?'

When she didn't answer for a moment, still shocked by the fact that he had bothered to get in touch, he went on quickly, 'I've been wanting to talk to you for a long time. I just didn't know how to say what I needed to say.'

Jassie recovered slowly. 'How are things with you? Are you still working just as hard as ever?'

'It's still just as hectic. Actually, though, I'm coming down to Cornwall for a holiday soon. I'm due some leave and I wanted to see you again. Perhaps we could meet up when I'm down there?'

'I...I'm not sure that would be a good idea...'

'Don't say no, Jassie...please, don't do that. I wasn't thinking of anything heavy...just dinner, maybe, one evening, and we could talk.'

Jassie bit her lip. 'I thought we said everything there was to say...'

'For old times' sake...as friends? Is that too much to ask?'

'I suppose not,' she said at last, giving in. She wasn't happy at the thought of seeing him again. She had the feeling that Rob wouldn't want to simply remain friends, and she wasn't ready to start over again with him. Too much had gone wrong in their relationship before. But because they had been so close at one time, she probably owed it to him to at least have dinner with him when he was in town.

Still uncertain that she was doing the right thing, she finished the call a minute or so later, as Alex came to join her.

'Are you all right?' he asked, searching her face with keen eyes that missed nothing. 'It wasn't an emergency call out, was it?'

'No...nothing like that.' She wasn't ready to talk to him about her relationship with Rob just yet. 'It was just...a friend, wanting to arrange a meeting, that's all.'

'You don't look too thrilled about it. In fact, I'd say you look as though you've had a shock of some sort.' His eyes were narrowed, a frown etching its way into his brow.

'Do I?' She floundered for a moment, then said quietly, 'It's probably just that I missed breakfast today. I really ought to go and get myself some lunch, and then I'll feel a hundred per cent better.'

'Are you telling me that you've worked right through to lunchtime without having anything to eat?'

'Well, yes. I overslept this morning and I didn't have time to stop for a break mid-morning, so there simply hasn't been time for me to get something.'

His mouth set. 'Come on,' he said firmly, taking her arm and practically lifting her off the bench in one fluid movement. 'I'm taking you to lunch right now. I can't believe you could be so senseless as to try to carry on without having had so much as a biscuit. Carole would have brought you something if you'd asked. You're a doctor, for heaven's sake. You, above all people, should know you can't hope to function properly on an empty stomach.'

'I was going to get something just as soon as we had finished here.'

Her protests were futile. Alex muttered something under his breath that she didn't quite catch, and that was probably just as well, judging by his grim expression. He whisked her over to his car and bundled her into the passenger seat.

'Would you mind telling me where we're going?' she asked mildly as he turned the car onto the coast road. 'You need to bear in mind that we have to get back to the surgery this afternoon in good time.'

'I thought we'd go to the Gallery restaurant on the promontory overlooking the sea,' he told her easily enough. 'Is that all right with you?'

'That sounds fine to me.' It wasn't too far from the cottage or the surgery.

'Good. That's settled, then.'

In a short time, they reached the cluster of buildings that made up the small centre of activity on the seafront. The Gallery restaurant was a small, attractively set-out place, with intimate little dining areas created by clever use of latticed wooden screens and discreetly placed foliage. The lighting was soft, and there were pretty table settings, with beautiful brocade cloths and flowers making a centrepiece.

The menu was extensive, Jassie discovered. Diners could choose from a wide menu of seafood, or vegetarian meals, or more traditional fare, and the appetising smell of good food that wafted on the air made her suddenly realise that she was famished.

Alex asked for a table by the window, which overlooked a glittering blue sea, and immediately they were seated the waiter took their orders. Jassie decided to settle for the more traditional menu, with a melon cocktail starter, followed by a deliciously crisp salad and freshly baked bread.

She looked around appreciatively. 'This is a lovely place,' she said, letting her glance sweep over the beautifully drawn sketches and original paintings that adorned the walls. 'Those landscapes look so lifelike, don't they?' There were watercolours and oil paintings that covered a wide range of settings, from rural to seascapes, and most of them were available for sale. 'If I were buying, I think I'd find it hard to decide which one to choose.'

'I'd probably settle for a seascape,' Alex said. 'There's something primeval and challenging about the sea, isn't there?'

'Do you enjoy battling with the elements?' The food was brought to their table, and Jassie spooned a tasty mouthful of cool melon and star fruit, savouring them thoughtfully. 'Is that what you like about the job?'

'Possibly,' he said with a crooked smile. 'Putting out to sea makes a vast change from sitting behind a desk at the surgery. In a way, it's invigorating, it makes me feel revitalised.'

Through the main course, they talked about some of the times he'd been called out to take part in rescue missions at sea, and she guessed that the crew of the lifeboat must think of him as one of their own.

'Aren't you ever afraid, though?' she asked. 'There

must have been times when you knew you were taking a risk.'

'Driving a car can be risky if the weather's bad and there's ice on the roads. It doesn't stop me from doing it.'

'But you don't think that I should be allowed to have the same choice as you?' Jassie delivered the words with a quiet challenge.

He made a face. 'Considering it was a new experience for you on the lifeboat, you did very well to cope the way you did. The conditions were awful out there, but I would have preferred it if you hadn't been there at all. I know what it's like to see someone hurt in a similar situation.'

'Was it someone close to you?' Her throat was dry all at once. She was suddenly unsure how she would feel if there was a woman in his life.

'My cousin,' he said. 'He was injured in an accident at sea, and the horror of that is with me all the time.'

'What happened to him?'

'He was hurt on a rescue mission. He had always wanted to work with the emergency services, and he hadn't long joined the lifeboat team when they went out to help pick up the crew of a capsized trawler. The rescue was going well, initially, but then there was an explosion and he was right next to where it happened. He could have been killed, so in a way it was fortunate that he escaped with his life. As it was, he lost the use of some of his fingers. There was nothing anyone could do to repair that damage.'

He paused and looked at her, his eyes dark and serious. 'So do you see why I feel responsible for you?

It's one thing to put myself at risk, and quite another to take on that burden for someone else.'

'It was a terrible thing that happened to your cousin,' Jassie said quietly, 'and I can see why you have doubts about having to be responsible for me. But, you see, that's where the problem lies, isn't it? You don't have to look out for me. You have to realise that, as adults, in the end we are all responsible for ourselves. You must stop thinking about the pros and cons and just accept that I'm here to do a job, and that I'm every bit as professional as you are.'

He made a rueful face. 'That's easier said than done.'

'Maybe, but I'm sure you can do it,' she said lightly. 'Anyway, in this day and age, you aren't allowed to discriminate between the sexes.'

'I know all the arguments about discrimination, and in the end you got the job because your qualifications and experience stood out over and above any of the other candidates, male or female. We're not allowed to be sensible and realistic in these days of political correctness gone mad.'

'I expect Dr Marriott met with your approval, despite the fact that she's a woman,' Jassie marked sniffily.

Alex threw her an oblique glance. 'She was a long-time friend of Dr Hampton, as a matter of fact, and she had been with the practice long before I came on the scene.'

'But you do agree that you need a woman doctor on the team to cater for the needs of some of your female patients?'

'I can't deny it, but I felt we needed someone who looked more physically capable, and I would have preferred someone who was actually already living locally. That way, there would have been little doubt about their staying power. That's partly why I insisted on the six-month clause.'

She'd guessed he'd been behind that. 'I'm not quite sure why you made an issue of it. It isn't really your problem, is it, in the long run? After all, Dr Hampton is the senior partner here, and he seems happy enough with my work. In the end, he's the one who'll decide whether I'm to carry on here, isn't he?'

He nodded. 'You're right. He is the senior partner...at the moment. But he's due to retire in a few months, and then that position will fall to me.'

Her lips parted on a small gasp. 'You're going to be the senior partner?'

'That's right.'

Trying to absorb that, she turned her attention momentarily to her salad, then said, 'I shall simply have to go on trying to prove myself, then, shan't I?' She grimaced, knowing that it wasn't going to be easy, given his deep-seated doubts. Shrugging off the matter, she said quietly, 'Tell me about your family. Do they live around here? What does your cousin do nowadays?'

'James works in a boatyard, in the office mainly, though he works on the boats sometimes, painting and adding the finishing touches. It's amazing how able he is, considering his accident.'

He smiled, thinking about that, then went on to say, 'My father's a senior registrar at the county hospital, specialising in neurology. He was deeply upset about what had happened, and the fact that very little could be done to restore the function to that part of his hand.'

'I can imagine he would have been.' She frowned, then asked, 'Does your mother work?'

'Yes. She works at the same hospital, but in the maternity wing. She's a midwife.' He finished eating, and caught the waiter's attention. 'Would you like a dessert?'

'Not for me, thanks. Just coffee.' She slid her fork into a mound of grated cheese. 'I suppose with that background,' she mused, 'you were bound to take up medicine.'

'It was what I always wanted to do, and it does help to have family around you, who understand what your work entails. I see my parents quite often, work schedules permitting. They have a house in Treen, not too far away from here.'

Jassie finished off the remains of her meal. 'That was delicious,' she murmured with a sigh of satisfaction. 'Though I don't know how I'm going to cope this afternoon. I'm too full up to do any work.'

He laughed, a throaty, huskily attractive sound. 'I'm sure you'll manage. Do you want to go back to the cottage for a while? We've half an hour or so before we have to be at the surgery, and we could perhaps take a walk along the beach.'

It only took a few minutes to reach the cottage, and as she stepped out of the car he said, 'Have you tried the path down to the beach from here yet?'

'Yes, last week. It's a lovely sheltered spot out here, isn't it? It's almost like having my own private stretch of sand. Once the weather picks up, it'll be bliss to go down there and sunbathe.'

'You could almost do that today,' he said with a smile. 'Last night's storm seems to have cleared the air, and there's hardly a cloud in sight. Do you want to take a walk down there now?'

'I'd love to. Do you know that you can see right across the bay from the end of the path?'

He nodded. 'I took some photos the last time I came to visit Eva Marriott and her husband. It's a hobby of mine. The only trouble is finding the space to store all the pictures.'

'I know what you mean. I'm like that with glassware. Every place I go, I find beautiful pieces, and I'm running out of shelves and nooks and crannies to display them.'

'I'd noticed you'd put your own stamp on the place. It looks great. You've made it homely and comfortable.'

'I love it. I love everything about it—the house, the location. My bedroom window looks out over the bay, and sometimes I just sit there and drink in the view. It's wonderful.'

The path down to the beach was to one side of the house, partially hidden from view by the overhanging branches of trees. It sloped at a fairly steep angle, and Alex reached for her hand to help her down. It was a natural, relaxed offer of assistance, but even so Jassie's heartbeat quickened in response.

His fingers closed warmly around hers and it felt for all the world as though a charge of energy was surging through her entire body. It was so distracting that she had to work hard to swiftly assemble her scattered wits and make her feet follow the path.

'Here we are,' Alex murmured a couple of minutes later, looking around with satisfaction at the sweep of golden sand that stretched for half a mile on either side.

They walked to the water's edge, where the sea rolled slowly in to shore and the waves broke in little bands of white foam on the beach. Jassie searched for shells, keeping to the firm, damp ribbon of sand where the water had retreated.

'Here's one for your collection,' Alex said, handing her a spiral shell that was perfect in every detail.

'Oh, it's beautiful, it's flawless,' she breathed softly, studying it with delight. 'I'll put it in my pocket so that I don't lose it.'

'I should watch out for that wave, if I were you, or you'll be going back to work with wet feet,' Alex warned, laughing, and she turned, wide-eyed, to look at the breaker that was coming in at a fast and furious pace.

'Where did that one come from?' she yelped, jumping quickly out of the way and colliding with Alex's solid frame.

'Same place as the rest.' He grinned, his hands going around her waist to swing her around and out of the way. Moving so quickly, she would have stumbled if he hadn't held on to her, and as the water flowed close up to his feet he stepped back, keeping her aloft.

'You saved me,' she said breathlessly. 'I would have been soaked.'

He smiled down at her. 'So I did.' He slid her

slowly back down to the ground, and as her softly feminine curves were gently crushed against the length of his body, her senses woke up in a wild flurry of disorder. The warm intimacy of that leisurely journey made the blood sing in her veins, and filled her head with dizzying sensation.

When her feet eventually touched the warm sand, her limbs felt weak and shaky, fluid almost, and she was glad of his hands resting lightly at the small of her back because without that gentle support, she was sure she might have fallen.

His gaze captured hers and held it for a long, heady moment before his arms circled her more firmly, keeping her near to him. She looked back at him dreamily, uncertain, yet so mesmerised by what was happening that she couldn't have resisted him if her life had depended on it.

Flame sparked in his eyes, and his glance moved to slowly trail over the pink fullness of her mouth. His hand shifted, gliding over the sensitive curve of her spine, stroking, caressing, causing sunspots of tingling awareness to flare into life wherever he touched her.

He muttered huskily, 'I just know that I'm going to regret this later, but...' His hand cupped her chin and lightly tilted her face so that her lips were just inches from his own. 'Heaven help me...I can't help myself...' Then his mouth brushed hers, and the featherlight touch was so achingly sweet that her heart thudded discordantly in response.

Jassie's lips parted, softened, yielded, and with a ragged groan he took her mouth again, deepening the kiss, tasting, seeking, with an urgency that made the blood fizz in her veins.

She hadn't known that she could feel this way, as though nothing mattered but to feed this hunger. Alex's body was hard and strong, pressuring her gentle curves so that her breasts were taut with need and heat pooled in her abdomen. Her mind swirled. Even with Rob, it had never been like this…

It was a disturbing thought, and she stumbled back a little, her feet sinking into the sand. What was she doing, letting her wayward senses get the better of her? Hadn't she learned enough to warn her against letting her heart rule her head?

Even so, his kisses drugged her senses, leaving her limbs languid and compliant, and she was helpless to do anything other than respond with equal passion. The sun beat down on her and she felt its golden rays lightly touch her skin, making her mind hazy with heat.

Perhaps that was it. She was suffering from a kind of sunstroke…because this was surely madness. She had to work with Alex. Wasn't it enough that he already thought she wasn't up to the job, without jeopardising her future by getting involved with him when he had so many doubts about her?

With a low moan, she fought temptation, dragging her mouth from his, pressing the flat of her hands against his arms.

'Jassie?' He resisted her retreat, moving with her, his lips tracing a searing path across her cheek, his warm breath fanning the slender column of her neck.

'Alex, stop...please...' she muttered unevenly. 'I can't do this...'

'Why, what's wrong?' he said huskily, easing back from her a little, banked embers still burning in his eyes. His voice deepened, becoming rough around the edges. 'I thought you wanted this as much as I did...' He searched her face, and the heat in his expression slowly died. 'It's Rob, isn't it? You're still thinking about your fiancé.'

'It's too soon. I...I don't think I'm ready for this. I'm sorry.' Her voice faded. 'I made a mistake.'

His brows met in a frown. 'I didn't think he was out of your life yet. There was something in the way you spoke about him.' His eyes narrowed on her. 'Was the phone call from him? Is that why you were looking so pensive earlier?'

She drew in a ragged breath. 'Was I? Look, time's getting on. Perhaps we ought to be heading back to the surgery.'

He blinked, as though he had no idea what she was talking about, but then he looked down at his watch.

'You're right,' he said at last. 'I'll take you back.' There was a coolness in his tone now, and Jassie turned away from him with a heavy heart and started to head back up the path towards the cottage.

CHAPTER SIX

'So...WAS it your ex-fiancé who called you this morning?' Alex persisted, as they reached his car.

Jassie pulled in a steadying breath. He wasn't about to give up, was he? And maybe it would be better to have it out in the open. 'Yes, it was Rob,' she admitted as she climbed into the passenger seat. She watched him turn the key in the ignition. 'He's planning on coming down to Cornwall for a holiday, and he wants us to meet up for dinner one evening.'

His brows met in a dark line. 'How do you feel about that?'

'I'm not really sure. It's taking me a while to get used to the idea. His call came out of the blue...I wasn't expecting to hear from him again.'

'Do you want to tell me about him?' He turned the wheel, easing the car onto the main road. 'How did you meet?'

'We met when I was working as a junior doctor in London...he was at a party at the senior registrar's house, and we hit it off straight away. I'd just finished a stint of night work and I was ready to let my hair down. And he was smooth, and charming, and fun to be with. He was exactly what I needed right then.'

'Was he?' Alex frowned. 'How?'

That was something she had tried to work out for

herself over the last few months. She needed to know where it had all gone wrong, to make sense of it.

She said cautiously, 'I was working hard and studying for specialist exams at the same time, and somehow he made everything easy for me. I found that I could relax with him, we had fun together. He was kind and considerate, and we seemed to be very well suited.'

She smiled a little, remembering that time. 'Rob was very good to me. He had a way of organising things so that I didn't have to worry about anything. He would even go out and stock my cupboards for me if I had been too busy to shop for food. He said he didn't work the hours that I did, and it was no problem for him.'

Alex glanced at her thoughtfully. 'He sounds like every woman's ideal man. What went wrong?'

'I think, after a time, I began to realise that he wasn't just helping me out. Bit by bit, he was taking over, until my life didn't seem to be my own any longer. He was deciding everything for me, and it got so that whenever I tried to put my own views forward there was an argument. After a while it seemed to me that we were constantly fighting over things that should have been simple to compromise on, and I got very tired of all the bickering. I'd started my GP training year by then, and I was on call a lot, quite often late at night so that I wasn't much in the mood for hassle of any kind.'

'So why did you stay with him?'

She was pensive for a moment or two. 'I think I felt for a long time that I was the one who was in the wrong. He persuaded me that I was working so hard that I wasn't seeing things in a proper light, and I really began to believe that my judgement must be flawed, as far as my life outside work went. At the time, there seemed to be so many good reasons why Rob's way was the best and he almost had me believing that I was being churlish to voice my objections. He said that once my career settled down, I would come to see the sense in what he was saying.'

'Didn't it occur to you that you had every right to your own opinions? You worked hard to be successful, and you achieved a professional status that should count for something? How could you let someone override you to such an extent?'

She made a face. 'I didn't think much about what I'd achieved really, apart from feeling a personal level of satisfaction. It's true, though,' she agreed, 'I was incredibly weak when it came to my personal life. I even let Rob choose where we were going to live when we were married. He insisted that he knew best about property, and I let him persuade me that he was right. I was foolish enough to go along with him.'

'I think perhaps you were more vulnerable than you realised at the time, and that's hardly surprising, given the circumstances. Junior doctors work very long hours, and I wouldn't blame anyone for wanting their life made a little easier.' His gaze narrowed on her. 'Maybe he hadn't totally persuaded you against your will about the house. There must have been something about it that appealed to you?'

She nodded. 'That's true. The kitchen was beautiful, and in the dining room there were patio doors opening out onto a small terrace. I thought that was a really attractive feature. It was a big house, though, and I wasn't too keen on that aspect. I think that's why Rob wanted it—he had the idea we might be entertaining his business colleagues. There were several guest bedrooms and he thought the executive setting was just right.'

Alex's brows lifted sardonically. 'Somehow "executive" doesn't sound at all your kind of thing.'

'No.' She gave a crooked smile. 'It wasn't my ideal, and I thought it was a lot more than we could reasonably afford. In the end, though, I went along with him on the decision because he was right in a way—it was central for both of us, and that seemed to be an important factor at the time. It wasn't exactly what I wanted, but we could have spent a long time looking around and I still wouldn't have found the perfect house. I thought that when I put my own stamp on it, it would probably be much more to my liking.'

Alex nodded, giving his attention to his driving as he swung the car off the road. Jassie was surprised to see that they had arrived back at the surgery already, and she waited quietly while Alex concentrated on manoeuvring the car neatly into his parking slot.

When he had done that, she shifted in her seat, disturbed a little by all the memories that were being brought back into focus. She was ready to get out of the car, her hand going to the doorhandle, when he turned to face her.

'So, what happened? You're not wearing his ring any longer.'

'We'd planned to marry when I finished my GP

training year, but as the months went by I finally began to realise that I was making a big mistake. He was taking over more—becoming almost domineering—and I wondered why I hadn't noticed that before. I tried to be more assertive, telling him that a lot of the decisions he was making affected both of us, and he should be taking my feelings into account...but it just led to more arguments.' She winced. 'Then I discovered that he was seeing someone else.'

He gave a grimace. 'That must have come as a shock. Didn't you have any idea what was going on?'

Her shoulders lifted and she straightened up a little. 'No, I didn't. I finished work early one day and went to his place to see him, but he wasn't alone.' She bit her lip. 'It was the final straw. I told Rob it was over, that it wasn't going to work between us. And to be honest, when that was done, I just felt great relief, as though a burden had been lifted off me.'

'But now he's been in touch with you again.' Alex's gaze narrowed on her, searching her face. 'Maybe it came as a shock to him to realise that you would consider breaking things off with him, that you would be strong enough to go against him. Now that he's had time to think things over, he might want to see if you could make a go of things the second time around.'

'It's possible, I suppose...and you're right, I am a stronger person now. I feel that I'm ready to do things my way, and take on new challenges. That's why I like being here at the Riverside.'

'Because of the lifeboat work, you mean?' He frowned. 'That was a hurdle in itself. Wouldn't it have been simpler just to be quietly assertive, instead of trying to meet everything head on?'

Her mouth made an odd little smile. 'I don't think so. For a long time I've been part of a couple, rather than an individual, and now I have to try to prove to myself that I'm truly independent. My judgement was badly flawed, and I need to know that I can put that right and rely on my intuition again. If I make mistakes in the meantime, then so be it... Hopefully, I'll learn from them, and at least no one risks being hurt except for myself.'

He shook his head. '"Hurt" being the operative word. Do I need to remind you that your mistakes include being almost flattened by a runaway crate?'

'Ah, but I came out of that unscathed, didn't I?' she said, tossing him a backward glance as she pushed open the passenger door and stepped out of the car. She started to head towards the surgery.

Alex scowled. 'Only just,' he muttered darkly, catching up with her as she walked through the main doors into the building.

Still smiling, and in a better frame of mind now that she had all that off her chest, Jassie left him to check his work schedule and went to find Carole in Reception. She felt ready to tackle the rest of the day's work with renewed vigour.

Carole had organised the afternoon list, and Jassie's first patient had just arrived in the waiting room. Collecting her bundle of patients' envelopes, Jassie said, 'Thanks, Carole. I'll see Mrs Thorne and young Emily now. Just give me a minute to get settled in my room, then send them through.'

Emily Thorne was just two years old, a timid little girl who clung to her mother as they came to sit down by Jassie's table.

'Hello to you both,' Jassie said brightly. 'What can I do for you today?'

'There's a small lump on her eyelid,' Mrs Thorne explained. 'I'm not sure whether it's about to burst.'

'I'll have a look at it.' Jassie searched in a drawer and found a paper mouse finger puppet to distract the child. 'Emily, can I see your eyelid, sweetheart? Oh, where did that mouse go? Did you see it?' Moving her hand behind her back, she hid the puppet from view, then lifted it up so that Emily followed the movement, intrigued. Jassie took the opportunity to swiftly check the toddler's eye.

'Yes, there is a sore spot, and it looks as though it's coming to a head,' she murmured, inspecting the lump. 'You could try bathing it with a warm flannel to help it along,' she murmured, 'but I'll give you some drops for it. These things can be a bit of a nuisance.'

'Thanks.' Mrs Thorne sighed. 'It's been one thing after another just lately. She had a cold, and then a cough, and now this.'

'It goes like that sometimes. I'll listen to her chest and see if everything's all right.' She picked up her stethoscope and showed it to Emily, letting her listen through the earpieces for a moment or two. The child giggled, hearing the noises going on inside her chest, and then allowed Jassie to listen.

'She's certainly very chesty just now,' Jassie said quietly to the mother. 'I'll prescribe an antibiotic to clear up the infection.' Jassie looked at Mrs Thorne searchingly, noting the shadows under her eyes and her pale features. 'Is there anything else I can help you with—anything at all that's bothering you?'

'No. I'm OK, thanks. I'm just tired after Emily's restless nights. If she doesn't get much sleep, no one in the house does.'

'I expect she'll sleep better in a day or so, once the medicine starts to take effect, and then you'll be able to get some rest. In the meantime, is there someone in your family who could help out by giving you a night off? A grandparent, perhaps?'

'My mother would probably babysit for me but, to be honest, I'd sooner have Emily close by when she's poorly. I shall be fine once she's her old self. She's normally a good sleeper.'

'That's something, anyway.' Jassie smiled and gave Emily the finger puppet, and the child left the surgery, happily dancing the mouse in the air as she held on to her mother's hand.

When Jassie had seen off the last of her patients, there was a tap on her door and Alex put his head round.

'Is that it for today?' he asked.

She nodded, and stretched lazily like a cat, easing the tension in her aching limbs. 'Just about. I've a few notes to log into the computer and then I'm off home.'

He came and leaned on the edge of her desk. 'Me, too. Then I'm going over to my parents' house for a family supper. It's not often our schedules coincide so that we get free time off together.'

'That's the trouble with both of them working in a

hospital,' she murmured. 'The hours can be unsociable. Same for GPs in a way, but not quite to the same extent.'

'True. What about the rest of the weekend? Have you made any plans?'

'Weekend?' She blinked. 'Heavens, it's Friday, already, isn't it? It's come around so quickly.'

He laughed. 'Do I take it that you haven't arranged anything, then?'

'I hadn't thought about it but, like you, I usually spend some time with my parents. Lazy and relaxing sounds about right to me, although I'll probably call in at the hospital to see how Alan's doing.'

He frowned. 'Actually, it was Alan I wanted to talk to you about. I thought maybe we could go and visit him together. I saw him yesterday, and I think he would appreciate a visit from both of us.'

She nodded. 'How is he?'

'His breathing had improved, but he was still very weak. His wife has been in to see him, and she's made arrangements to look after him when he's well enough to be discharged.'

'That's good, isn't it? At least it gives them a chance to iron out some of their problems.'

'That's true. Natalie always said he worked too hard, so this way he doesn't have any choice but to rest.'

'So, did you want to visit him tomorrow afternoon? Aren't you meant to be on call this weekend, though?'

'I have to take the Saturday emergency surgery for a couple of hours in the morning, and then I'm on call, but I'll probably have some time free in the afternoon.

That might be the best time to go and see him, if you're agreeable?'

'Sounds OK to me.'

'I'll come and pick you up.'

Alex drove her to the hospital as planned, and Jassie asked, 'What kind of morning did you have?'

'Not exactly brilliant,' he said with a wry smile. 'I've just been doing the rounds. A few cases of food poisoning...people throwing up all over the place. Yuck. I think it's probably down to some mussels that had gone off, but the environmental health people will track it down.'

She grinned back at him. 'Somehow that makes me glad I'm not on call today.'

'There was one good thing, though. I checked on young Amy while I was in the area. She's home from hospital now, and doing nicely.'

'I'm glad. She's a sweet little girl, but obviously she was very poorly when I saw her.'

'Well, she was OK this morning, playing with her friends in the front garden and chatty as ever. It's certainly good to see her up and about again.'

They made their way to Alan's ward, where they found him propped up in bed with several pillows. There was a little more colour in his cheeks than there had been previously.

'How are you feeling?' Jassie asked.

'A bit odd, really,' Alan said, making a face. 'My limbs feel like lead, as though they're too heavy to move. I hadn't expected that.'

'You've been through a difficult time,' Alex told

him. 'Pneumonia is a serious illness, not something you're going to get over in a matter of weeks.'

'I know you're right,' Alan murmured. 'I'll probably feel better once I'm back in my own home.' He made a wry smile. 'The trouble with being in hospital is that you never get any rest. They wake you up at an unearthly hour, and they're clattering around the rest of the time with cleaning, and trolley rounds and what have you...and then the doctor arrives and wants to come and prod and poke.'

Jassie laughed. 'It sounds as though you could do with some peace and quiet. Have they said when you might be able to go home?'

'Monday or Tuesday probably, depending on what the consultant says when he has a look at me. I keep telling them I can read my own charts and decide I'm fit enough to be discharged, but they don't listen.'

'Just as well, from the look of you,' Alex murmured. 'You might think you're OK, but you need a couple of days more to be properly fit.'

They stayed with him for about half an hour longer, but left before he became too fatigued.

'He'll be glad to get out of there,' Jassie said. 'People usually feel happier convalescing in their own homes, don't they? And at least Natalie will be there to keep an eye on him.'

Alex took the road that led towards the seafront and parked by the harbour wall. 'Do you want to take a walk along the front for a while, maybe do a bit of window-shopping? It's a beautiful day, and it seems a shame to spend it indoors. Sometimes I think I spend so much time cooped up in the surgery that I long to come out and stretch my legs and breathe in the sea air.'

'I'd like that,' Jassie agreed. 'Maybe there's a boutique where something will catch my eye. I need to think about presents for the family. There are a few birthdays that fall this month.'

'Have you heard from your brother yet?'

'From Nick, you mean?' She shook her head. 'Nothing, up to now.'

'I'm sure he'll turn up, sooner or later. Perhaps he's looking around for a new job and visiting different parts.'

They got out of the car and walked along the seafront, taking in the view of the wide beach and the craggy headline that jutted out to form a sparkling bay. Higher up, on the rugged hillsides, little whitewashed cottages crowded together, with narrow, cobbled alleyways winding in between.

'This is such a pretty place, isn't it?' she murmured appreciatively.

He raised a dark brow. 'A lot different to the sort of place where you were going to live after you were married?'

'Oh, yes,' she said with a little grin, 'definitely that.'

'Do you think you'll want to buy a house of your own at some point? I can't imagine you'll want to rent for ever.'

'That's true. I'll have to give it some thought. It might be too early to rush into anything just yet. I still have to complete the six months' tenancy before I can approach Dr Marriott about buying.'

'You might not want to do that in a few months'

time. You may decide that you want to settle in another place...or even go back to London, perhaps.'

She frowned. 'What makes you think that?'

He shrugged. 'It happens. People think the grass is greener somewhere else, and then they find that they made a mistake.'

He said it casually enough, but his words had a sobering effect on her. Why was he even thinking along those lines? Was it simply that he didn't want her here? Once he became senior partner, he could take on whoever he felt would be best for the practice, and it could be that he had made up his mind to persuade John Hampton not to renew her contract.

Disappointment washed over her in a sudden tide. She had hoped that by throwing herself wholeheartedly into her work he would realise that he needed her there as part of the team, but it didn't look as though her plan was going to succeed.

They walked on, and he pointed out landmarks on the way, telling her a little of the history of the place. She tried to take an interest in what he was saying, but her mind was preoccupied now and it was difficult for her to concentrate.

When they reached the headland overlooking the beach where the surfers congregated, it dawned on her that there was something of a commotion on the sand below them. She frowned, peering down over the rail to see what she could make of it. A small group of onlookers had gathered.

'The lifeguard's down there, working on someone,' Alex said. 'It looks as though there's been an accident of some sort.'

She said quietly, 'Maybe we should go and see if there's anything we can do to help. We ought to at least find out if he needs us.'

He nodded, and shouted down to the lifeguard, 'Do you need any help down there? We're both doctors.'

The lifeguard looked up at them and nodded. 'I think this man's had a heart attack,' he called back, and Alex started towards the steps that led down to the beach.

'The emergency kit's in my car,' he told Jassie. 'Do you want to go back and get it while I go and see what's happening?'

'Yes, I'll do that. Give me your keys.'

He tossed them to her, and she took off at a run while Alex made for the beach.

Making haste was vital, and as soon as she reached the car Jassie wrenched open the door and slid behind the wheel. She would drive back to the beach and take the kit down from there.

On her return, she saw that the man was lying unconscious on a towel in the shelter of the headland, and the lifeguard was working desperately with Alex to revive him. Alex was doing compressions to the heart while the lifeguard was giving mouth-to-mouth respiration.

Jassie hurriedly unlocked the boot of the car and pulled out a defibrillator and the rest of the resuscitation equipment.

She raced over to the two men and knelt down beside the patient.

'Is that machine charged?' Alex said.

'It's charging now.' She worked quickly to set up

an intravenous access line. With that done, she took over from the lifeguard and inserted an airway to help their patient breathe. Putting the ventilation bag in place, she asked the lifeguard, 'Can you operate this for me?'

'Yes. I'll do it.'

'Good.' She moved back to Alex, who was straddling electrodes across the man's heart.

'OK.' He reached for the pads. 'Ready? Clear.' The shock to the heart wasn't enough to start it again, though, and he tried twice more.

It still wasn't working, and Jassie hurriedly gave the man adrenaline, praying that it would give him the added boost he needed. 'OK, give it another go,' she said, shifting back out of the way.

The sound of an ambulance siren reached them as Alex tried again, and this time the monitor recorded a sudden jerky response.

Alex breathed a sigh of relief. 'That's it,' he said exultantly, after a while. 'We've done it. We've got a good heart rhythm now.'

Jassie grinned with him, and the lifeguard gave a thumbs-up sign, sharing in the sudden release of tension.

'I'll go and meet the ambulance,' he said, getting to his feet. 'The paramedics will need to know where we are.' He left them, taking the steps up to the coast road at a fast pace.

There was nothing more they could do for their patient until the paramedics arrived so Alex started to pack the equipment away. 'Our patient looks stable enough for now.' He smiled at her, a warm attractive smile that instantly melted her insides. 'You were great,' he said. 'We worked well together, didn't we?'

'We did.' She smiled back at him, kneeling back on her heels, happy all at once because the sun was shining down on them and the world suddenly seemed bright and full of promise.

Then Alex leaned forward, flame sparking in the depths of his eyes. He reached for her and kissed her hard on the mouth, a swift, fervent kiss that sent the blood soaring wildly through her veins.

Dazed, Jassie responded instinctively, her lips parting beneath his, every fibre of her being coming alive as he plundered her soft mouth, deepening the kiss. She could feel the pounding of his heart against her breast, and distantly she registered the way his hands curved possessively around her arms. His lips were warm and firm, enticing her to respond with equal fervour, to cling to his with aching need.

She pressed her trembling fingers to his chest, wanting more but dazed by the way her senses were spiralling out of control. He held her, and it was just as well because without his steadying hands she was sure she would have swayed under the sheer intensity of that kiss. Then, reluctantly, he dragged his mouth from hers.

When he finally released her, she stared up at him, her blue eyes showing utter confusion.

Around them, a low ripple of gentle laughter and murmured appreciation came from a small crowd of onlookers, and Jassie's mind went into a spin. She had completely forgotten that anyone else was around, and now she felt a tide of colour flood her cheeks.

She sent Alex a fulminating glance. 'Why did you do that?' she whispered crossly. 'What must people be thinking?'

He made a crooked smile. 'Does it matter what they think?' he murmured under his breath. 'It seemed like a perfectly good idea at the time, and you did look beautiful and deliciously kissable just then.' His golden eyes teased her.

'It wasn't a good idea,' she told him.

'No...?' He looked doubtful, shaking his head. 'Well, maybe you're right, maybe it wasn't—not out here on the beach anyway, in full view of anyone who happened to take a passing interest. Still...' He laughed softly. 'It felt good while it lasted. Very good.'

'That wasn't what I meant,' she said through her teeth, a sense of outrage fizzing through her because he was making fun of her reservations, but her anger was wasted on him. Humour glinted in his eyes as he turned away from her to check their patient and then look towards the steps a few yards away.

The paramedics were approaching with a stretcher, and Jassie went hot all over again, imagining what they might have seen if they'd arrived just a minute or so earlier. It was bad enough having the tourists agog, without having their colleagues looking on as well.

Alex, utterly professional now, brought the paramedics up to date on the man's condition and helped them to transfer him to the ambulance, while Jassie hid her inner turmoil by dealing with all the equipment that needed to be taken back to Alex's car.

She was seething at the way he had reverted so quickly to a businesslike mode. He had lit the fuse on every nerve ending she possessed and now, just a moment later, he was calmly in charge of himself again, as though nothing had happened. It was quite clear how easy it was for him to turn his emotions on and off like a switch. The whole episode meant nothing to him. It had all been just a momentary flash of exultation, sheer joy that they had saved their patient's life, as far as he was concerned.

'He was lucky you two happened along when you did,' the lifeguard said.

'Not so lucky to have a heart attack in the first place,' Alex commented pithily. 'Though, to be frank, he doesn't quite look like a man who exercised all that often, and I suppose that's half the trouble. People might be couch potatoes most of the year, then they try to cram all their sport and leisure activities into a couple of weeks when the holidays come round.'

'Perhaps the answer to that is to have more holidays,' Jassie said drily. She hoped that their patient would do well from now on, and they could be thankful, at least, that they had done what they could for him.

They said goodbye to the lifeguard, and walked back along the coast road to where she had parked Alex's car.

'I need to go home,' she told him. 'Will you drop me off at the cottage?'

'So soon?' Alex cast a deceptively idle glance her way. 'It seems a shame to lose such a beautiful afternoon.'

'I promised I'd go and see my family this afternoon. They complain that they don't see enough of me.'

His glance narrowed on her, but he didn't try to persuade her otherwise, and she was glad of that. Her feelings were too raw right now. It hadn't meant anything to him, that kiss—it had just been a spur-of-the-moment expression of sheer elation. It was different for Jassie. She was beginning to care too much for him, that was the trouble, and she simply wasn't sure enough of her instincts to allow them free rein. She needed to be clear-headed and know what she was getting into, especially where Alex was concerned.

Deep down, she knew that he was a man who could turn her life upside down, someone who could quite easily steal her heart if she gave him half a chance. And there was the rub, because if she let him he could just as easily break it into little pieces...and how would she ever recover from that?

The next few days passed in a flurry of activity. The surgeries were busy with the added intake of tourists to the area at the start of the main holiday season, and on top of dealing with those Jassie was gradually taking over the child health clinics.

All in all, it was hard work, and she wasn't sorry when her appointments were all done one evening and she was able to tidy up her desk and get ready to go home. She walked through to Reception.

'Oh, there you are, Jassie,' Carole said. 'Are you all finished here for now?'

'All done for today.' Jassie nodded.

'That's good. You've a visitor, by the way,' Carole

murmured. 'He's been waiting in the coffee-lounge for you for the last fifteen minutes or so. Says his name's Rob Cassidy. I think he's travelled down here from London today, so I've given him coffee and biscuits to keep him going.'

Jassie frowned. 'Rob's here? I wasn't expecting him to arrive until tomorrow, let alone come here.' She tried to gather her thoughts. 'Thanks, Carole. I'd better go and find him.'

Rob was standing by the window, looking out over the paved quadrangle, when she went into the lounge, but he turned as she walked into the room and she stared at him, her mouth going suddenly dry. He looked pale, his features faintly drawn, and she wondered what had caused the strain that showed on his face. Was it their break-up, or something more?

She hadn't known how she would feel when she saw him again, but now her heart began to thud with a strange anxiety.

'Hello, Rob,' she said quietly. 'Did you have a good journey?'

'It was fine, thanks. I couldn't wait to get here, to see you again.' He looked her over, his hazel eyes taking on a warmth that she remembered from the early days. His dark hair was slightly longer than usual, but he was as smartly dressed as ever, in grey trousers and blue shirt, topped with a suede jacket.

'You look tired,' she said, seeing the shadows around his eyes. 'Perhaps you ought to have spent some time winding down instead of rushing over here.'

'I didn't want to. I booked in at a hotel and unloaded my luggage, and that was it. I decided to come and find you.'

'I didn't realise you knew where I was working,' she said unevenly.

'I got in touch with your family—I needed to contact Nick about some work he set in progress before he left, and your mother mentioned that you had a new job.'

'Did you find my brother?'

'Yes, eventually. Apparently he's interested in applying for a job in the London area, and he wanted a reference from our managing director.'

'I've been trying to find him, to talk to him myself, but he seems to have changed his number.'

'I expect he'll be in touch before long.' He walked towards her, his gaze never leaving her face, and before she had a chance to realise his intention he had taken her in his arms and was kissing her soundly on the mouth.

Stunned, she registered the kiss, and her mind went blank for a moment, then swirled crazily as she heard a sound behind her.

'Excuse me.' Alex's deep, cool voice startled her into shocked awareness of what was happening. 'I left my jacket in here.'

She pulled away from Rob in confusion, and turned to see Alex stride across the room to retrieve his jacket from the back of a chair. She couldn't read the expression in his eyes, and he went out without saying another word. The door closed behind him, leaving a draught of cold air to flow around her and settle like a chill mesh of steel on her limbs.

She wanted to go after him, but she couldn't move. Her mind and her body were frozen in time, and all she could think of was that Alex had gone and she was alone with Rob.

CHAPTER SEVEN

ROB broke the silence. 'I thought you might like to eat out tonight. There's a restaurant I passed on the way down here, just a few miles down the road. It looked the sort of place you would enjoy. Shall we try it?'

It was just as though nothing had changed. Rob had come back into her life as though he had never left, and Jassie simply felt numb inside.

'All right,' she said at last, her voice unsteady. 'I think perhaps it would be a good idea if we talk. A restaurant seems as good a place as any.'

Rob looked as though he was taken aback by her lack of enthusiasm, and maybe that was just as well. He thought he could come here as though nothing had happened, and everything could go on as before, and she needed to let him know once and for all that it wasn't to be.

'I don't know why you moved so far away from all that you were used to in London,' he told her later, over a meal and a bottle of wine. 'There was everything you could want there—the city life, the theatre and dining out, the parties we had with all our friends.'

'They were your friends,' she murmured, sipping her wine and feeling the dry bite as it slid down her throat. 'I don't miss any of it, Rob. I'm happy at the Riverside.'

'You only think that because you felt that you needed to get away, and that's my fault. I let you down, I realise that. You were working so hard, and we were arguing, and I turned to Rachel for comfort... But that was a mistake, Jassie. It didn't mean anything. It's you I want.'

'I don't find it that easy to forgive and forget,' she said quietly. 'You can't just turn the clock back and have everything the way you want it. Things have changed. I've changed.'

He was sober, listening to her, and she felt that he was at least making an effort to take on board what she was saying. As the evening came to a close, though, she felt a growing confusion. He wanted to see her again, to keep on talking and try to make sense of their break-up, and some of the things he said struck a chord with her.

'You were working so hard,' he murmured. 'I respected that. I wanted you to do well, and I was proud of you when you passed all your exams with flying colours and you achieved everything you set out to do. I did what I could to make things easy for you, but after a while it was as though you didn't need me any more. Perhaps that's why I turned to Rachel. She saw that I was hurting, and she soothed my ego. I was a fool, I know that, and I'm not trying to make excuses for what I did. I'm just trying to explain how it all went wrong.'

'I didn't feel that you gave me enough room to be independent,' Jassie told him. 'I didn't think you were listening to me any more.'

'We were both wrong. We handled things badly,

and I think we should at least talk things through now that the heat of the moment is all behind us. Can't we do that, Jassie? Can't we spend some time together, just for old times' sake? I'm only down here for a short spell, and there's no harm in a few dinner dates, is there?'

'Maybe not.' Because of all that they had shared in the past, she agreed that they would have dinner again some time soon. It wouldn't hurt to sort things out between them now that time had healed the initial shock of their break-up. After all, as he pointed out, he would be back in London at the end of the month, and by then they might both be in a better frame of mind.

Back at the surgery the next day, Jassie made an effort to concentrate on the job in hand, but it was difficult. Alex had hardly said a word to her since their afternoon at the beach, and she couldn't fathom what was going on in his mind. There was an atmosphere, a tension between them that hadn't been there before.

Frowning, she looked up as her door opened and her last patient of the morning came into the room. She recognised Simon, the crewman from the lifeboat, and she greeted him warmly.

'Hello, Simon. What a surprise to see you here.' Then she saw that he had a little boy with him, a child about four years old whose features bore a strong resemblance to Simon. 'Is this your little boy?'

He nodded. 'That's right. This is Daniel.'

Jassie smiled at Daniel, who gave her a baleful look in return so that she guessed he might be the one who needed the consultation. 'Your daddy told me how much you liked going on his boat, Daniel. It's lovely to meet you. How are you?'

'I felled over,' he said with a frown and a puckering of his lips. 'And it was Jamie Collins's fault. He tripped me up in the playground and made me hurt my shoulder.'

'Did he? Oh, dear. Does it still hurt?'

Daniel was thoughtful for a moment. 'It does if I bang it,' he said truthfully.

Jassie looked up at his father. 'Is it Daniel's shoulder that you've come to see me about?'

'Yes. He actually hurt it a couple of weeks ago—he fell on it, from what we can gather—but we thought he'd just had a knock and that was all there was to it. He can move his arm without any problem, and it hasn't seemed to bother him too much unless, as he says, he catches it against something. My wife checked him over this morning, though, and she found a lump which worried us.'

'I'd better have a look.' Jassie turned to Daniel. 'May I see your shoulder, Daniel? Will you slip your shirt off so that I can see if you've bruised it?'

The little boy did as she asked, and Jassie gently manipulated his arm through a range of movements to check that all was well. After a minute or two, she said thoughtfully to Simon, 'That seems to be OK. I can't find any problem there. But you say there's a lump...would you like to show me where it is?'

'It's just about here...' Simon trailed a finger lightly over the child's clavicle, and Jassie carefully examined the area he pointed out.

'I can feel it,' she murmured a moment later. 'All

right, Daniel. That's fine, thank you. You can put your shirt back on again now.'

While he was doing that, she told Simon, 'It looks as though he might have broken the bone when he fell, but it has probably started to heal already. What happens is that where the bone mends it becomes stronger, and the lump you can feel is that healing process beginning. I'll give you a form to take along to the hospital so that he can have it X-rayed to be sure. I doubt that they'll want to bind it up, but they'll probably give him some painkillers to make him feel a bit better.'

'Broken?' Simon looked as though he had been delivered a hammer blow. 'It was broken? And all this time we thought he'd just bruised himself…' He shook his head, trying to take it in. 'The poor little chap hardly even cried…' He turned to his son and brushed his fingers affectionately through his hair. 'You're a brave little fellow, aren't you?' he said wonderingly.

Daniel's cheeks dimpled in agreement, his eyes widening thoughtfully, so that Jassie guessed he was going to make the most of this for some time to come. His parents weren't going to forget in a hurry either, and she could imagine that Simon was already planning a treat to make up for what the little boy had been through. She smiled at the pair, and thought bleakly how wonderful it would be if all troubles could be dealt with so easily.

She wrote out the X-ray form and handed it to Simon. 'There you are. Just hand it in at the X-ray department at the hospital, and they should see you straight away.'

'Thanks, Jassie.' He shook his head again, still not quite taking in what had happened.

She walked with them to Reception, where Alex was sifting through a mound of post. He looked up, acknowledging Simon and Daniel with a smile as they came up to the counter, and they chatted for a while until Daniel became fidgety.

'We'd better be on our way to the hospital,' Simon murmured, adding with a rueful grimace, 'I just hope that there aren't too many people waiting there already.' Before he left, though, Simon turned back to Jassie and said quietly, 'Are *you* all right? You didn't seem to be quite yourself when we first walked into your room.'

'Didn't I? I may have been preoccupied, that's all.' From his expression she saw that he didn't believe her, and she added lightly, 'Thanks for asking, anyway.'

'Well, if you're sure? If there's ever anything I can do for you, you know where to find me.'

'Thanks, Simon. I'm fine, honestly.' She was touched by his offer, and it made her realise all the more how much she liked being here in this little corner of the world. Perhaps it was working in the lifeboats that brought Simon and others like him together as a community. People were friendly and caring, they helped one another out, and she valued that more than anything.

Simon and Daniel went out, and Alex sent her a narrowed glance as she went to get her jacket. 'Did Simon hit the nail on the head? Is something wrong?' he asked in a clipped tone. 'Did things not go as well with your fiancé as you might have hoped yesterday?'

'I wasn't hoping for anything,' she murmured, turning away from him to search in her bag for her car keys.

'Weren't you? Perhaps you're forgetting that I saw the way you reacted to him. He had only to hold his arms out to you and you were there with him as though nothing had happened.' There was an edge to his voice, a harsh cynicism that grated on her nerve endings. 'If his coming back here is going to change your way of thinking, I need to know about it. It could affect your role here.'

'It won't,' she muttered tersely. 'Why should it? I've already told you what happened between Rob and me, and that it's over between us. He's just here for a holiday, a break from all the stress at work. A lot has been going on within the company lately and he needed to get away. I'm not surprised, really... I thought he didn't look too well, and the strain seems to be showing.'

'You're kidding yourself, aren't you?' He grimaced. 'Perhaps you don't want to admit that you know the real reason he's here. He came after you, and he must have had in mind more than just a friendly visit.'

She made a quick sound of denial and he gave a gesture with the flat of his hand to cut it off. 'Look, you don't have to go on the defensive about this. I know what you told me, about why you broke up, but that doesn't mean you can't change your mind about the situation. You're bound to have regrets about what happened.'

'I made a clean break from all that by coming down here. I didn't expect him to turn up out of the blue.

It's thrown me, that's all. It's unsettling, and I need some time to get used to the idea that he's here.'

'And when you do, I can see what's going to happen. A few months down the line from here, you'll be going back to him and I'll be looking to take on another doctor.' His mouth twisted. 'I knew all along that your appointment here was a mistake. I should have worked harder to persuade John to change his mind about employing you.'

His tone was cutting, and she was bitterly hurt that he could so easily dismiss all the work she had done at the Riverside up to now, as if it was of no account. 'How can you say that? I've done nothing to give you cause to regret me being here. You've absolutely no reason to believe that I'm not up to the job. I've worked hard, and I've built up a good relationship with my patients. You've no legitimate reason for complaint in anything I've done so far.'

'I didn't say I had. What I'm saying is that I don't have any confidence that you'll still be around at the end of your contract. I've been down this route before with young women doctors who get a notion to work in a pleasantly rural practice and then find that they miss the cut and thrust of the city. You're no different. You fancied a change and you thought you'd try a toe in the water and maybe that would make your fiancé think twice about what he was missing. It worked, too, didn't it? He didn't wait long before he came to find you.'

'I'm wasting my time, having this discussion with you, aren't I?' she said tightly. 'You're not listening to anything I say. I gave you my reasons for wanting to work here before I started the job, and they haven't changed one iota.'

It hurt bitterly that Alex could turn things around and accuse her of being fickle, simply because Rob had arrived. Her mouth tightened. 'You have no right to question my motivation. Besides which, as far as I'm aware, Dr Hampton is still the senior partner here, and he's the one who still makes the final decisions. If I have any queries about anything to do with my work, I'll sort them out with him, not with you. At least that way I can be sure of getting a fair hearing, and not one clouded with chauvinistic attitudes.'

She turned swiftly away from him, and as she started to head for the door he called after her, 'Is that it? You're just going to walk out and leave it at that, are you?'

Jassie swung round and sent him a glare. 'I'm going out, to get a breath of fresh air. The atmosphere in here right now is stifling.'

Feeling angrier than she had in a long time, she swept out of the health centre and headed for the car park, taking time to pull in a few long breaths and restore a modicum of calm before she drove off.

Alex was out on call when she returned an hour or so later, and she was glad about that. Her mood was still fractious, and it wouldn't have boded any good for either of them if he had been around.

In the evening, she went home and moved restlessly about the cottage, tackling some of the household chores. Had she gone over the top with Alex earlier? Perhaps she was more tense about Rob's sudden arrival than she realised, and the stress was beginning to show in her reactions. She would need to keep a firmer check on her emotions.

Some time later, as she was fixing herself a toasted sandwich, the doorbell chimed and she wondered who on earth would be calling on her at that time of the evening.

Opening the door, she was startled to see Alex standing in the porch, and her mouth dropped open in surprise.

He said drily, 'Before you shoot me down in flames, I should say that I'm not here to pick a fight.'

She lifted a quizzical brow. 'Of course you aren't.'

She drew back to let him in, and as he stepped into the hall he sniffed the air appreciatively. Jassie frowned, then said in a rush, 'Oh, I completely forgot. I'm making toasted sandwiches...'

She made a dash to the kitchen and retrieved her supper from the cooker just in time. Alex followed, looking around her small kitchen.

'Look, Jassie,' he began, 'about this morning...'

'Let's forget about that, shall we?' she murmured.

'It isn't that easy. Rob coming back here is bound to change things.' He put up a hand as she made to cut in. 'Hear me out, please. As you said, him turning up out of the blue was a shock to you, and I know you have to come to terms with that. I just don't want to see you getting hurt, that's all.'

'I can take care of myself,' she said, her chin lifting. 'You don't need to try to protect me.'

'If you say so.' He looked doubtful.

'I do,' she said firmly, then busied herself putting the toasted sandwiches onto a plate. 'Would you like one?' she asked. 'I made extra, and I was probably being over-generous. I'm sure I won't have room for all of them.'

'Thanks,' he accepted lightly. 'If you think you'll have enough.' He sampled the hot sandwich and murmured appreciatively. 'Mmm...this is good.' He smiled. 'My mother reckons I'm a bit like a Labrador we used to have at home. I'm never quite sure that I'll get my meals when I hope for them, so I eat up whenever it's on offer, just in case.' His mouth tilted attractively. 'Perhaps I burn up too much energy.'

'I can imagine,' she said, her gaze warily skimming his long, lean figure. He was wearing the grey suit that he wore in the surgery, and it looked good on his tall, broad-shouldered frame. *He* looked good. She couldn't quite get used to the fact that he was actually here in her kitchen, as large as life, warm and vital, and his nearness was having a disturbing effect on her. All her earlier anger melted away.

'Aren't you on call tonight?' she asked.

'I am.' He bit into his sandwich, savouring the hot bacon filling, and added quietly, 'Actually, that's why I'm here. I had a call from Sarah...the girl you met at the Harbour Inn. You two have become quite friendly over the past few weeks, haven't you?'

Jassie nodded. 'We have. Is she all right?'

'Not really. She called the surgery, complaining of abdominal pains, and she was asking if you would be able to go and see her. I know you're not on call, but I wondered if you might want to go with me on this one? She sounded quite anxious, and I think a woman's touch might be useful here. It's entirely up to you, of course. I know it's annoying to have to go out just as soon as you have a meal ready. I'll understand if you don't want to go with me.'

'That's all right. I like Sarah, and I don't mind at all, especially if she's asking for me.' She frowned. 'Does she have any other symptoms?'

'She's been vomiting, but there's no diarrhoea.'

'Did she mention Sam? Is he all right?'

'She didn't say anything about him. She sounded as though she was in pain and didn't want to talk much at all.'

'From the sound of things, we ought to get over there as quickly as we can. I'll go and get my coat.'

'Thanks, Jassie.'

Within minutes they were in Alex's car, heading for the village where Sarah lived in a pretty colour-washed cottage with clematis rambling over the walls and porch.

Sarah struggled to answer the door when Jassie rang the bell, and Jassie could see straight away that she was suffering from strong pains.

'I'm sorry to call you out,' Sarah managed to say as she let them in. Beads of sweat had formed on her brow, and she was holding her abdomen as though that might ease the pain. 'I tried to get by on my own, but it's getting worse.'

'Let me help you into the living room,' Alex said, going over to her and lending her a supporting hand. 'From the looks of you, you did right to give us a ring.'

'Try and lie down on the settee and make yourself as comfortable as you can,' Jassie murmured. 'I'll examine you to see if we can find out what the problem is.' She opened her medical bag and drew out a thermometer. 'Pop this under your tongue for me, will you?'

Jassie made a quick examination, gently seeking out the site of the pain, and when she had finished she said quietly, 'Your temperature's high, and we need to get that down. I'll do a urine test to make sure, but I think you're suffering from a kidney infection, Sarah. I can give you some tablets to take right away, and I'll write out a prescription for you. Is there anyone who can go and collect it for you?'

Sarah shook her head. 'I'm on my own here, with Sam. Jack...my husband...is working away for a few days. I tried to phone him, but I couldn't get in touch. He must have his mobile switched off or something. That's why I didn't know what to do. I don't know how I can manage until this pain goes away. I need to take care of Sam. He's in bed just now, but tomorrow...'

'I know,' Jassie said soothingly. 'Don't worry. We'll sort something out for you.'

Alex went out into the hall and came back with a small address book. 'Is his number in here?' he asked, flipping through the pages.

Sarah nodded, and subsided into the cushions as another wave of pain swept over her. 'He's working for an agency. I spoke to them, and they said they would try to get in touch with him. He's working at a small town in Devon.'

'I'll try to contact them again and see if they made

any headway,' Alex murmured. 'Lie back and rest, and leave everything to us.'

Jassie went to the kitchen and came back with a jug of water and a glass. 'Swallow these tablets, and then I'll go and check on Sam,' she said softly. 'I can stay with you until Jack gets here, if need be, so you don't need to worry about a thing.'

'I managed to talk to someone from the agency,' Alex said. 'They've been in touch with Jack and he's on his way.'

It was about two hours later when Jack finally arrived home and he went over to his wife right away and put his arms around her. 'My poor Sarah,' he murmured gently. 'I'm here now, it's OK. I'll look after you.'

'Make sure she drinks plenty of fluids,' Jassie said as she and Alex finally took their leave of them. 'She should be feeling better in a few days, but she ought to stay in bed until then.'

'I'll take care of everything,' Jack promised. 'I can't thank you enough for taking care of her.'

Outside, the night sky was dark and the stars were out in force. 'I hadn't realised how late it was,' Jassie said, yawning and squinting down at her watch as she slid into the car beside Alex.

'Do you wish you'd stayed at home?'

She shook her head. 'Oh, no. I'm glad I went with you to see her. It would have been difficult if you'd been called out to another patient. She would never have managed on her own.'

'That's true enough. It's a pity her brother doesn't live closer. I know she has friends who would have helped out in the morning, but it was the immediate situation that called for action. You were a great help, and I was relieved that you were with me. So was Sarah. If Sam had woken up, he wouldn't have been too upset about her illness if he'd seen that you were there, too.'

He manoeuvred the car into the lane that led away from the village, and just then Jassie's mobile rang.

She frowned. 'This is a strange time of night for anyone to be calling.' She put the phone to her ear, and then exclaimed, 'Nick…heavens, is it really you? I've been wondering when I would hear from you. What happened? Why haven't you been in touch? How could you leave it so long?'

'Sorry about that,' her brother said. 'I've been really busy, chasing up new job opportunities, and in the meantime I changed my phone and forgot to give out my new number.'

'Well, it's good to hear from you, even if it is late.' Jassie laughed.

'Not quite so good, I'm afraid,' Nick said quietly, and she sobered immediately at his tone. 'I was actually calling to pass on some news about Rob. We've spoken to each other recently…something to do with work…and I phoned him tonight to follow up on it, but he's been taken ill. He's been admitted to your local hospital, an emergency admission, and I thought you would want to know.'

'In hospital?' Jassie said. 'Why? What's happened?'

'I'm not sure of the details, except that he collapsed earlier this evening. I heard that he's been having blackouts lately, and after this latest one they decided to admit him for tests.'

'Oh, no…' She was finding it difficult to absorb the news, but she took in a shaky breath and said, 'Thanks for telling me, Nick. I'll go and see him right away. Will you promise me that you'll keep in touch?'

'Of course.'

She cut the call and stared blankly ahead for a few moments, until Alex said in a concerned voice, 'What's wrong, Jassie? Is it something to do with your family?'

'Not my family. It's Rob. He's been admitted to hospital after a collapse.'

His expression darkened. 'I'm sorry.' He glanced obliquely at her, his features shadowed. 'Do you want me to take you over there to see him?'

'Are you sure you don't mind?' Her voice was thready. She was still trying to take on board the fact that Rob was ill…Rob, who had always seemed so strong. 'It's late, and I don't know how long I'll be…'

'You're in no state to go there alone,' he said firmly. 'You've had a shock, you're trembling. I'll go with you.'

'Thank you.' She subsided back into her seat, all the energy draining from her, and neither of them said much more as Alex turned the car towards the town.

Rob had been admitted to a side ward, and the nurse on duty was reluctant to let him have visitors at that time of night, but after some persuasion she relented.

'You can have five minutes, that's all,' she warned.

'Thank you. I won't disturb him, I promise.'

Jassie turned to Alex, but he forestalled her by saying quietly, 'You go in and see him. I'll wait out here for you.'

'OK. Thank you for being here with me.' She pulled in a deep breath, bracing herself, then pushed open the door and went into the room. Rob was lying in bed, wired up to a heart monitor, and Jassie saw that he was being given medication through a drip into a vein in his arm. He was awake, but he looked ghostly white and drained of energy.

'How are you?' she asked softly.

'Oh, I'm not doing so badly,' he murmured tiredly. 'The doctors say they need to check out my heart.' He winced. 'Something about the…' he paused, trying to get his breath '…electrical impulses not being conducted properly. That could explain all the dizzy spells I've been having lately.'

'Don't talk if it tires you,' Jassie said gently, concerned at his lack of colour. She reached for his hand and covered it with her own. 'I just wish I'd known what was happening. I'm so sorry to see you here in hospital.'

He didn't answer for a moment, his eyes closing, and she was afraid that he might be on the verge of collapse. Then he said in a faint voice, 'It's good to see you here, Jassie. Thanks for coming.'

'I had to come and see how you are.'

Just then the nurse put her head round the door, and said firmly, 'You must leave him to rest now.'

Jassie nodded. 'I'll come and see you again tomorrow,' she told him, leaning over and kissing him gently. 'You take care.'

The nurse was holding the door open, and Jassie

could see Alex waiting in the corridor outside, his expression serious as he watched her walk towards him.

'How is he?'

'Not too good.' She grimaced. 'He looks as though he could fade into unconsciousness at any time. It sounds as though the sinoatrial node in his heart isn't working properly. His heart rate is very low.'

He nodded. 'I had a word with the nurse. They're giving him isoprenaline to try to bring the rate back up again.' He put an arm around her shoulders. 'You look as though you've had just as much as you can take for one day. Come on, I'll take you home.'

'Thanks, Alex.' It was a comfort to have him near, to know that she could lean on him and that he wouldn't let her down. He was calm and considerate, and his gentle manner was almost her undoing. She felt weepy all at once. It was probably that she was overtired. 'I feel as though I'm to blame for what happened. Perhaps if we hadn't split up, he might have been more able to cope.' Her mind had been racing over the last hour or so, filled with worries that she might have done something to bring about Rob's illness, that she could have precipitated his condition through adding to his stress.

'You mustn't blame yourself. You don't know what could have brought on his heart block. He's a young man still, but there could have been some history of myocarditis, or some other problem that we don't know about yet. Certainly it wouldn't have been anything that you did. You're just thinking that way because you're over-emotional right now.'

'I suppose you could be right.'

He walked her over to his car and settled her in the passenger seat. It was dark now, and as they set out for home the lights from passing traffic intermittently pierced the gloom.

'Look, I'll take you to my house,' he murmured. 'It's nearest and, besides, I don't think you should be alone tonight. You're still shocked and trying to take it all in.'

'All right. Thanks.' Jassie gave in easily enough, feeling unutterably weary and wanting nothing more than to close her eyes against all the hassles of the day. Tomorrow, perhaps, she would feel stronger, but for the moment, having Alex close at hand sounded just about right.

His house was set back along a leafy lane, the wide porch brightened by a pool of golden light that welcomed them.

'Through here,' he said, taking her inside, an arm around her to gently shepherd her through. She caught a glimpse of a neat oak-fitted kitchen before he led her into the living room.

Even though she was weary, Jassie saw that it was a homely, spacious room, furnished tastefully in pleasing shades of summer, with two comfortable sofas invitingly adorned with soft scatter cushions.

'Go and sit down in the living room,' Alex said. 'I'll make us some tea.'

He came and joined her a few minutes later, placing a tray of tea and sandwiches down on a glass-topped coffee-table. 'Try to eat something. It's a long while since you've had anything, and it might help give you a bit more stamina.'

They sat together on the settee and talked until the early hours of the morning. She was worried about Rob, miles from home and desperately ill, and Alex did his best to soothe her. Jassie leaned back into the cushions, content simply to hear the sound of his deep voice, absorbing the closeness, the warm feeling of having him near. She gradually became drowsy, and he drew her close, his arm going around her, nestling her into the shelter of his body. She rested her head against his chest, feeling safe and secure, strangely unwilling to move, a deep languor sweeping over her.

She must have fallen asleep like that, because some time later she was vaguely aware that she was alone. Now that Alex had gone she felt oddly chilled.

'Alex?' She frowned, mumbling his name, not liking the fact that he had gone. It had felt so right having him by her side.

'I'm here,' he said. 'It's all right.' His voice was wonderfully soothing, like hot chocolate sipped slowly so that the warmth spread to fill every cold and empty part of her. He leaned over her and she lifted a hand to him, her fingertips resting on the smooth wall of his chest so that she felt the suppleness of his skin through his shirt and registered the steady, reassuring thud of his heartbeat.

She said faintly, 'I thought you had gone and left me. I didn't want to be alone…'

'I didn't go far away—I just went to fetch a duvet to cover you. I ought to get you to bed really, but you looked so cosy lying there.'

'I don't want to move,' she admitted sleepily, and he carefully laid the duvet over her, his hands brushing her body as he tucked it in. Every nerve ending she possessed sprang to tingling life.

'Stay with me?' she asked huskily.

'Of course.' His voice was rough around the edges and, though he spoke gently, there was a remoteness in his eyes that she hadn't seen before.

'Is something wrong?' she asked. Then, on an afterthought, she added with a quick gasp, 'You haven't heard anything from the hospital while I was sleeping? Rob's not had a turn for the worse, has he?'

'No, Jassie, I've heard nothing at all,' he said quietly. 'I'm sure Rob's in good hands and he'll be fine. Go back to sleep.'

CHAPTER EIGHT

ALEX had made a start on breakfast when Jassie walked into the kitchen next morning. The smell of freshly made coffee floated on the air, and the table in the corner of the room had been laid in readiness. There was a rack of toast at the centre, along with butter and preserves and a jug of orange juice.

'Can I do anything to help?' she asked.

He turned around from the hob where he was deftly scrambling eggs, and said easily enough, 'There's no need.' He waved a hand towards the table. 'Go and sit down and help yourself to whatever you want.'

He looked wonderful, his shirt open at the neck to reveal the lightly bronzed column of his throat, and his dark trousers emphasising the long line of his legs. She felt a lump in her throat as she studied his tall, familiar figure. She wanted to go over to him and lean her head on his broad chest, feel the reassurance of his arms around her, but he looked so brisk and efficient that she was suddenly uncertain as to how he would react.

Instead, she said quietly, 'Thanks for being with me last night. Everything that has happened lately has been such a shock, and it knocked me for six, I think. First Rob coming down to Cornwall, and then him being taken ill. I couldn't quite take it all in.'

He gave a taut nod. 'That's understandable. He was

a part of your life for a long time, he meant a lot to you. It would have been unnatural if all this hadn't affected you.' He spooned a mound of creamy egg onto toast and pushed the plate towards her. 'Eat up, before it gets cold.' He glanced at her keenly. 'What do you plan to do today? Are you going back to the hospital?'

'I thought I would phone first and see how he is, and then go and visit as soon as soon as I'm free at lunchtime. With a bit of luck I'll have a couple of hours before my afternoon appointments start.'

'I can pull in your morning surgery for you, and we could get a locum in to take over the rest of your workload for the next few days. It probably wouldn't serve any good purpose if you go into work. Your mind won't be on the job. You'll only be worrying about what's happening to Rob.'

She bit her lip. 'It'll be too difficult for you, with Alan still away, won't it? I want to go to Rob...he looked so vulnerable last night, shocked and ill, and I feel I need to support him just now, but I don't want to leave you in the lurch. I know it isn't easy to get hold of a locum at this time of year.'

'We'll manage,' he said distantly. 'I'll have a word with Dr Hampton and explain the situation to him. I'm sure he'll understand and want us to help you in any way we can. Besides, I think I know someone who can step in for us. A friend of mine from medical school has just moved into the area. I know he's looking around for locum work to tide him over for the next month or two, so I'll give him a call.'

'That would solve the problem, wouldn't it...if he

agrees? It wouldn't be for long, just a couple of days maybe, until Rob's over the worst...'

'Don't worry about it.' His gaze was unreadable, and she couldn't be sure whether he was simply being dismissive or whether there was more behind his subtle withdrawal from her. 'You want to be with him, and that's all that matters. Take as long as you need.'

She picked up her fork and trailed it over her food, making tracks through the fluffy egg. Alex was handling this in a matter-of-fact way, and that ought to make her feel much more positive about things, but she couldn't help feeling that he was irritated by the situation. Could she blame him for that? After all, she had only been with the practice for a relatively short time, and now she was leaving them short-handed just at the beginning of the holiday season.

'I just feel that I can't leave him to face this on his own,' she explained tentatively. 'His family are in Spain just now, and there's no one he can rely on to be with him and help him through this. I have to do what I can. I just don't like to think of him alone and vulnerable.'

'I told you, Jassie...I understand.'

She nodded, hoping that he really did understand. She would help Rob through this, and when he was well again she would gently nudge him towards getting on with his life without her. For the moment, she didn't feel as though she had any other options.

They finished breakfast and Alex drove her back to the cottage, dropping her off with scarcely a backward glance. That hurt. She wanted him to hold her, to kiss her and make her know that everything between them was fine, that the warmth and depth of feeling she had known before in his arms was still hers. But instead there was nothing, and she didn't know how to deal with that.

Rob's condition hadn't improved much overnight. His heart rhythm was still being monitored, and Sister Kennedy, who was in charge of his nursing care, told her, 'We'll need to observe him for a while longer, you understand, but it's becoming quite likely that he'll need to have a pacemaker fitted.' She made a face. 'I'd prefer it if he was a little less anxious. He seems to be agitated about something, and it isn't helping his condition. Do you have any idea what it could be that's bothering him?'

Jassie winced inwardly. It probably hadn't helped that he had travelled all the way down here to try to renew their relationship, and things were still unsettled between them, but she wasn't about to confide that to the nurse. Instead, she shook her head, murmuring, 'I could talk to him for a few minutes, if you like, and see if I can do anything to settle him down.'

'I think that would be a very good idea.' Sister Kennedy beamed her approval. 'He seems much more peaceful when you're around. Just a few minutes, though...we mustn't let him get over fatigued.'

Rob's lips moved in a faint smile when she went into his room. 'Jassie...I was beginning to think I must have dreamt you were here last night. I was afraid you would go away and not come back.'

'I wouldn't do that,' she told him quietly, going to sit beside his bed and taking his hand in hers. 'I want you to get well, and I'm going to be hanging around until you're on you're feet again.'

'Thanks, Jassie. You're a treasure. I don't deserve you, I know that, but I'm so glad you're here.'

He squeezed her hand, and then with a small sigh he closed his eyes. Jassie watched him, concern edging her lips. She still cared about him, as a friend, and it hurt badly to see him suffering this way. He needed her right now, and she had to be as supportive as she could be, but would he get the wrong idea?

Would he believe that their relationship was back on its old footing? He was in no state to be told the plain truth now, obviously. Hearing bad news could only make his condition worse, and she didn't want to be responsible for prolonging his illness. Sooner or later, though, she would have to find the words to tell him that she only wanted to be his friend.

She rang Alex that evening to fill him in on what was happening.

'Hello, Jassie,' he murmured. 'How are things? Is Rob any better?'

His voice was deep and calm, soothing like warm honey. If she could just be with him, touch his hand, feel his nearness... anything to take away the memory of their cool, remote parting this morning.

'They're going to fit him with a pacemaker. The operation's scheduled for the day after tomorrow so, unless there's a problem, I'd like to stay close by until I know that he's on the mend. Is that all right? I tried to phone Dr Hampton to explain things, but I wasn't able to reach him.'

'He was at a meeting for most of the day. There

isn't any problem, though. I managed to get cover. Craig Ellis is coming in to take over your workload. He was glad of the chance to join us. We got on well when we were students, so he fits in perfectly, and he's an excellent doctor, so you needn't have any worries about your patients. Take all the time you need.'

'Thanks,' she said huskily, then added, 'How did your day go?'

'Well enough. I called on Sarah to see if there's been any improvement, and it does look as though the infection's responding to treatment. Oh, and your little patient, Daniel, had broken his clavicle, as you said. Simon came in and told me that the X-ray showed a clean break, which has started to heal.' He made a soft sound in his throat. 'Daniel's fine, by all accounts, but Simon still hasn't recovered from the shock.'

She smiled faintly. 'It'll take a while.'

'Keep your chin up over there,' Alex said. 'I know it can't be easy.'

'I'll do my best.'

It was hard, talking to him from a distance, not being able to see his face and read his expression. When the call was disconnected, she felt oddly out of sorts, almost as though her roots had been severed. It was a lonely feeling.

She went into the surgery next morning on her way to the hospital, hoping for the chance to see him, to talk to him even if it was just for a few minutes, but Alex had already gone out on an emergency call. Disappointment washed over her.

'Dr Ellis is dealing with your list of patients this morning,' Carole told her. 'He seems to be coping very well, and he's fitted in beautifully, just as though he's been here for ever.'

'I'm glad,' Jassie said. 'It helps if things run smoothly, doesn't it?'

'It does.' Carole smiled, and glanced at Jassie's holdall. 'Are you on your way to the hospital again?'

'Yes. I've been to Rob's hotel and picked up a few things for him—pyjamas, soap, towel, that sort of thing. Everything happened so quickly, I didn't think to do it straight away.'

'It must have been a shock for you.'

'Yes, it was, and I was worried about what would happen here at the surgery if I had to leave suddenly to be with him, but Alex was wonderful. He organised everything, and told me to just concentrate on being with Rob. I can't see many other practices being as understanding, given that Rob isn't a relative.'

'Well, he was your fiancé, and that counts for something, doesn't it? Besides, it must have helped that Alex had already drawn up a short-list of names for a doctor to fill the upcoming vacancy...not that it's time yet, of course, but he wanted to be prepared.'

A chill swept through Jassie's limbs. 'Vacancy?' she echoed.

'Oh, nothing's cut and dried yet, is it? But it doesn't hurt to have a few options up your sleeve, just in case. At least, that's Alex's way of thinking.' The bell rang for Dr Ellis's next patient and Carole quickly turned her attention to the list of patients. 'Mrs Blakeley, would you like to go through to Dr Ellis's room, please?'

A patient came to the reception window, wanting to

speak to Carole, and Jassie realised that she was holding her up. 'I can see you're busy,' she said huskily. 'I'll...I'll talk to you later, Carole.' She went to the door, her mind in a daze.

Was Alex already planning to replace her at the Riverside? How could he do that, without even talking to her about it first?

Somehow she managed to get through the rest of the day, putting on a bright face and talking to Rob at the hospital as though nothing else mattered but that he concentrated on getting well.

His heart rhythm had stabilised sufficiently for a permanent pacemaker to be fitted, and the operation was to take place the next day as planned.

Jassie made sure that she was with him when he received his preparatory medication next morning, and she stayed with him until he was wheeled off to Theatre. Then, feeling slightly at a loss, she decided to take a walk in the hospital grounds.

It was a bright, sunny day, and the air was fresh, with just a slight breeze blowing. Flowers were in full bloom all around and Jassie was stunned by the beautiful display they made. Looking around, she tried to take it all in. The weeks had gone by so quickly. How had the time slipped by without her noticing?

She walked slowly along the path that curved towards a pretty terraced area, where a couple of bench seats had been placed in a prime position to catch the full rays of the sun. Sitting down, she gazed unseeingly ahead, her thoughts running back over all that had happened these last few months.

It had been April when she'd first gone to work at

the Riverside Medical Centre, and now there were just a few short weeks before her trial period would be over. And then? What was going to happen after that? Would she still have a job?

'Jassie? Sister Kennedy told me that you were out here.'

The familiar, deep voice intruded on her reverie, and she looked up, startled to see Alex standing by the bench. The sun glinted over his long, lean frame, lighting his features, and his smile, in turn, warmed her heart. It was as full of affection and caring as ever, and her spirits lifted at the thought that he had taken the trouble to come and find her. How could she ever have doubted him?

'Alex…' she said breathlessly. 'I didn't know you were coming. You didn't say…'

'I wasn't sure whether I would be able to get away, but Alan phoned up and said he wanted to come back to work.'

'He did? Is he well enough? I would have thought he needed longer to get his strength back up.'

'He wants to ease himself back into work gradually, just doing the odd few hours. He has too much time on his hands at home, and I think he was feeling a bit out of it. This might be the best way round the problem, letting him take a couple of surgeries a week. We can monitor how many hours he's doing, and keep a close eye on his health at the same time.'

He came and sat down beside her on the bench. 'How's it all going? You said Rob was having his operation today.'

'Yes, he's in Theatre right now. I'm just praying that it will all go well. No complications or anything.'

He searched her strained features, then put an arm around her and hugged her close. 'It's a simple enough operation. I'm sure he'll come through this without any problems.'

'I know. It's silly of me to get myself in a state about it.' It was like coming home to find herself in his arms once more, and she snuggled against him, the joy of having him here warming her through and through. It was just as though he was her own special pool of sunlight. Deep down, she had always believed that he was a man she could rely on, and the simple fact that he was here made her heart sing.

She curled her hand around his. 'How long can you stay?'

'Only a short time, I'm afraid. I just wanted to see that you were bearing up all right. I have to get back to be on call for the lifeboat. Alan isn't strong enough to cope with it, and Craig isn't used to that kind of work. He'd manage, I'm sure, but it isn't fair to expect it of him.'

'I should be there, helping you…'

'Don't even think about it,' he said forcefully. 'You've enough on your mind already.'

They sat together in the warm sunshine for a while longer, until they heard footsteps approaching and Jassie looked up to see Sister Kennedy coming out to the gardens. She straightened, bracing herself for news of Rob.

'I thought you might still be out here,' Sister Kennedy said. 'I've come out for a breath of air myself. Mr Cassidy's back from Recovery, and you can go and see him now if you like. He's asking for you.'

Anxious all of a sudden, Jassie felt the heat drain from her skin. She stood up, aware that Alex rose with her. 'Is he? Is he all right? Has he recovered enough yet to be able to see anyone?'

'He's as well as can be expected at this stage. I think he'll be very glad of your company, though, now that he's feeling a bit more responsive. You seem to have the knack of soothing him.' Sister Kennedy settled herself down on the other end of the bench, and stretched her legs out in front of her. 'Oh, to get the weight off my feet for a while!'

Flustered, Jassie looked up at Alex, but his expression was shadowed, revealing nothing of his thoughts to her.

'You go and see him,' he said. 'I have to leave, anyway.'

'Do you?' The warm intimacy of the last few minutes dissolved as though it had never been, and Jassie could have wept. She was torn, wanting to be with Alex but knowing that she had to make sure that Rob was all right.

Alex walked with her towards the building, stopping at the entrance where double glass doors led to the wards.

She put a hand on his arm. 'Thanks for coming to see me, Alex,' she mumbled, her voice breaking a little. She was touched that he had taken the time to be with her, and now, impulsively, she moved closer to him and reached up to kiss him lightly on the mouth.

For an instant, he was very still, but then he tugged

her close to him and kissed her swiftly, a brief, incandescent flame of a kiss so that she felt the sweet intensity of it reverberate throughout her body.

Jassie wanted to cling to him to make the moment last, but it was over almost as soon as it had begun. He put her away from him and she stared up at him dazedly, not understanding the look of regret, of self-reproach almost, that crossed his features. He shook his head as though to clear it.

'You'll be OK,' he said. 'You'll get through this all right. When you're finished here at the hospital, we'll get together to sort out what your plans are.'

'About when I'm coming in to work, you mean?' she asked doubtfully. 'It shouldn't be too long, now. Days, rather than weeks, I'd have thought...perhaps a couple of days at the most.'

'You may find that you need longer than that. Rob seems particularly vulnerable right now, according to what Sister Kennedy was telling me, and I can see for myself that you're pulled in all directions. Take your time, and make sure that you feel comfortable with whatever you decide. Either way, let me know.'

'I will. I know it must be difficult for all of you at the Riverside.'

'It's fine. We're all keeping on top of things.' As an afterthought, he added, 'By the way, Dr Marriott phoned the surgery this morning and asked me to remind you about the lease on the cottage. There's only a month to go, she says, and you'll need to decide what you're going to do about it when the lease runs out. If you don't want to renew it, she's thinking of putting the cottage up for sale. Either way, she wanted you to give it some thought and maybe give her a ring later.'

Jassie frowned. 'I'm not sure what I ought to do about that yet.' More than anything, she wanted to stay on at the cottage, to buy it even, but it all depended on what happened once the six-month trial period at the Riverside was over. If she knew for certain that her job was going to be safe, then she could consider putting in an offer for the cottage.

'You don't have to give her an answer right away. She can wait a couple of weeks. She just wants you to weigh up the pros and cons. As things are, you can't be sure what you'll want to do in a month's time.'

'I do know what I want. I want to stay on at the Riverside.'

'Perhaps you think you do now, but you've been through a mighty upheaval this last week, and things haven't settled down yet. You could well change your mind. Rob's arrival here has thrown a spanner in the works and you need to take time to think things through.'

Alex's words made her reel. How could he talk so casually about her not staying here?

'I don't understand,' she said in a strained voice. 'I've already told you what I want to do, that I want to go on working at the surgery, and you don't seem to be taking that on board.' She looked at him searchingly. 'Is it that you don't really want me to stay on here?' Had Carole unwittingly revealed the truth, that he was already working to find her replacement?

'I just mean that nothing's set in stone, and you need to take some time to think things through before you make a final decision. It's early days yet, and you're only just getting used to the idea that Rob is making a recovery. You can't be sure what it is that you want. You came down here to make a fresh start and perhaps now that you've had the chance to reassess your life, you might be ready to go back to what you knew before...a city practice, a lively, thriving community.'

She was stunned by his words. 'It seems to me that you're the one who's having second thoughts. You're not accepting that I know my own mind.' She frowned. 'Is this all because of Rob? Do you think I shouldn't have taken so much time out to see him when he was first taken ill—is that it?'

'Of course not. You needed to be with him. You and he were more than just friends, and it's natural that you would want to be together. I just feel that your emotions are mixed up right now, that's all.'

'And what about us?' she asked in a small voice. 'You and me? Have I been wrong in thinking that there was a spark of something between us? Every time you held me in your arms I thought you wanted me, cared about me,' she said huskily. 'I thought there was something between us that was more than simple friendship, something that was worth holding on to. Was I wrong to think that?'

'Perhaps I made a mistake, and made you read more into it than there was,' he said bluntly. 'The fact is, Jassie, we have to work together...for the time being at any rate, and it's no good if our relationship keeps getting in the way. It's never a good idea to mix work and pleasure, is it?'

She blinked, trying to take in what he was saying. *For the time being.* What was that supposed to mean? And how could he be so casual about something that had been so precious to her? Had all her instincts been so utterly wrong when she had thought their feelings for each other went deeper than a mere surface affection?

'A mistake?' she echoed. 'Is that what you think it was?'

'I do.' His tone was measured, flat. 'Whatever you might have thought we felt for each other, it happened too quickly, and I should have seen it coming and put on the brakes.'

Jassie listened to him and felt sick inside. Just a short time ago he had made her feel secure, wanted, protected, and her world had seemed almost perfect. Yet now the chill tide of reality was flooding in on her, and she was left wondering how on earth she could have laid herself open to a rejection like this.

Had it all been just a purely physical thing on his part? He had wanted her, but now he'd had a change of heart and he was already regretting their closeness. As far as Alex was concerned, all he had been looking for had been an uncomplicated, no-strings affair, with no angst on either side. Then, when the time came for her to leave, there would be no recriminations, no looking back.

She straightened her shoulders. 'You're right,' she muttered distantly. 'We have to work together. Why make it more difficult than it need be?' She turned away from him, muttering, 'I'll call you and let you know what's happening…when I'll be coming back to work.' Blindly she pushed her way through the double doors and escaped into the cool anonymity of the hospital corridor.

It was too late for him to start reasoning things out in a cool and practical fashion. She had already lost her heart to him, and he had shattered it in little pieces. She would never be the same again.

CHAPTER NINE

Rob was feeling groggy after the anaesthetic, but he was glad to see Jassie. 'They're going to keep me under observation for a day or so,' he said, 'to make sure that the pacemaker's working properly. After that they think I should be good as new. Well, almost.' He gave a wan smile.

'I'm glad you're OK,' she said softly, taking his hand in hers and squeezing gently. 'Really glad.'

She stayed with him, talking to him about his operation and trying to reassure him that he really should have a new lease of life now that the pacemaker was in place. She sensed that he had doubts, and guessed that the whole episode had left him confused and uncertain, though he wouldn't have admitted it for the world.

'What's going to happen now?' he asked tentatively. 'Will you be staying around, now that it's all over?'

She hadn't expected the directness of that question, but she took a deep breath and nodded. 'I shall stay around and make sure that you're completely well. I want to be sure that you can cope on your own,' she told him gently. 'It's been difficult for you, being away from home, away from your friends and family, and that must have made things doubly awkward for you.'

'But you don't want me as part of your life any

more, do you?' Rob's intent gaze held hers, and she wished she couldn't read the desperation that was in them.

'Rob, this isn't the time for this kind of discussion,' she said huskily. 'You need to concentrate on getting your strength up.'

He smiled grimly. 'I suppose I knew all along that it wouldn't work, me coming after you. I left it too late... I made a mess of things, didn't I?'

'You didn't do anything wrong, Rob,' she murmured. 'It's just that you need someone more in tune with your way of life, someone without a demanding career who can add her weight to your ambitions. I'm too stubborn and independent to ever have made you a good wife, you know. But I am your friend...I'll always be that. I'll always be glad of the good times we had, the happy moments we shared...and there were a lot of those, weren't there?'

'Just not enough to keep you with me,' he said sadly.

They talked awhile longer, until Sister Kennedy came back from her break and insisted that Rob needed to rest. Jassie took her leave of him, kissing him lightly on the forehead and promising that she would be back to see him tomorrow.

He nodded, smiling ruefully. 'Tomorrow, then.'

Sister Kennedy was checking her message pad at the nursing station as Jassie went out. 'It looks as though his family are on their way to see him later today,' she murmured. 'They've had to travel some distance, but they should be here around teatime. That should cheer him up.'

'Yes, it should.' Jassie nodded, and wondered if the sister understood a lot more of what was going on than she cared to reveal.

The next day, when she visited him again, his parents and his sister were with him, and she could see that he was looking much brighter, much more able to cope. She went back to the cottage late in the afternoon, feeling much more reassured with the way things were going.

Now that Rob was on the mend, she could get her own life back on track. She phoned Dr Hampton at the surgery, to update him on what was going on.

'It's good to hear from you, Jassie, my dear,' he said cheerfully. 'I'm so glad that your friend is feeling better. All this must have come as a dreadful shock to both of you.'

'It was, and it was very considerate of you to let me take the time out to be with him. I must say, though, that I feel much more confident about leaving him now. He seems so much better now that his heart rhythm is more stable.'

'That's good news. I'm really pleased that everything turned out well in the end. So...you say you feel he can cope without you being at his side now. Does that mean you'll be coming to see us at the surgery? We've missed you.'

'Yes. I thought I would come back to work on Monday, if that's all right with you?'

'That's excellent news. Monday's fine. Alan's taking several surgeries now, and we have Dr Ellis with us to take the weekend home visits, so there are no problems there.'

'Good. I'm glad that's all settled.' On a more cautious note, she added, 'There is something else that's on my mind, though. I need to talk to you about my six months' trial period coming to an end. I'd like to stay on, but I need to know what you think about that.'

'You know I want you to stay with us, Jassie. I've said so all along. You're a good doctor, and an asset to the practice, and Alex knows my views on that…but you know you really need to talk him about this. He'll sort everything out for you. I'm taking more of a back seat now.' He chuckled. 'There comes a time when you have to give the youngsters a chance to shine and, as you know, I've been letting Alex handle most of the administration side of things for a while now. Have a word with him when he gets back.'

'Isn't he there with you now?'

'No. Unfortunately, he was called out to go with the lifeboat a few hours ago. There's a ship on fire, just offshore, and the lifeboat has to stand by to take the crew off. There are helicopters to ferry the wounded to hospital as far as I know, but Alex is there, helping out as much as he can. It's a nasty business…there have been reports on the local news all afternoon.'

His words filled Jassie with sudden dread. 'Have you heard from Alex? Is he all right?'

'I can't help you there, Jassie, I'm afraid. I haven't heard anything for the last hour. I would have thought it must all be over soon, though.'

He rang off a short time later, and over the next couple of hours Jassie tuned in to the news programmes, searching for any information that would give her some clue as to what was happening. What she heard, though, didn't make her feel any easier.

Explosion on board... Ship being towed out to sea... A number of casualties... The snatches of explanation made her heart thump erratically. Alex was there in the middle of it all. What if he was hurt? What could she do? How could she find out what was happening to him?

The questions crowded in on her until, hating this feeling of helplessness, she drove down to the lifeboat station to see if she could glean any more information from there.

The boat hadn't returned yet, though, and no one seemed to know any more than she did. Surely the crew would be heading for home by now? What was keeping them? Hadn't they been able to get back to shore?

Perhaps they had changed course and put in at a different port some miles away...that might be it. She would ring the landlord at the Harbour Inn to find out...not from here, though. Waiting around here just served to increase her sense of frustration.

Instead, she took the car into the village, parking alongside the common. She walked over to a wooden bench and sat there to make the call.

'Sorry, my love,' the landlord said. 'I know how worried you must be. I've been listening to the news myself. But they haven't put in here, not yet at any rate.'

'Will you let me know if you hear anything?'

'Of course I will. I'll give you a ring.'

There was a café nearby and Jassie went over there

to buy herself a coffee and sit for a while by the window, watching the gulls circle overhead and swoop down from the rooftops in search of scraps of food. It was difficult for her to concentrate on anything. All the while there was a feeling, gnawing away inside her, that something was very wrong.

She drained her cup, then went outside to pace along the pavement, unable to bear the tension that was building up inside her any longer. Finally, in desperation, she drove down to the lifeboat station once more, and her heart missed a beat when she saw that the boat was back.

A crowd had gathered, milling about various members of the crew, and she searched the faces keenly, looking for Alex. He was nowhere to be seen.

Luckily, Simon was there to field her anxious enquiries. 'He isn't here, Jassie. I'm sorry...I hate to be the bearer of bad news...but he was injured. They've taken him to the hospital.'

'Oh, no...' She felt the blood leave her face. 'What happened to him? How bad is it?'

He shook his head. 'I don't know. I wish I could tell you more, but I was working with some of the ship's crew, helping them on board the lifeboat. All I heard was that he had dragged one of the men to safety and was trapped when fire swept through the hold. He was taken off in the helicopter. I haven't heard anything more than that.'

Jassie's breath came out in a shuddery gasp. 'Oh, no.' Her mind was in a whirl, and she could hardly think straight. 'I must go and find him, see how he is.' Shakily, she added, 'Thanks for telling me, Simon.

What about you? Are you all right? Were any of the lifeboat men hurt?'

'We're all OK, Jassie. The crew of the ship didn't fare so well, but at least we got them all off.'

Trembling with apprehension, her legs as weak as water, she hurried back to her car and drove to the hospital some seven or eight miles away. Alex had to be all right…he had to be.

'I'll make enquiries for you, Dr Radcliffe,' the receptionist said, when Jassie arrived at the hospital and breathlessly asked about Alex's condition. 'I believe the doctors are with him right now.' The woman picked up the phone and dialled, and for Jassie the wait seemed interminable.

Impatiently, she started to pace again. She didn't want to have to stand here, filled with dread. She wanted to see him now, to see for herself what had happened to him.

'He has been moved to a side ward apparently,' the receptionist said at last, putting the receiver down. 'He suffered burns to his shoulder, back and hand, and he also inhaled some smoke, but he has been receiving treatment and he is a little more comfortable now. You can go along to see him, if you like,' she added kindly.

If she liked… Jassie hurried along the corridors, desperately trying to control her breathing. She had to try be calm, she had to prepare herself to be supportive, to do whatever she could to help him. Oh, why did this have to happen to Alex?

She wasn't at all sure what she expected to see when she arrived at the ward, but when she opened the door into the room her eyes widened at the scene that met her.

Alex was sitting, tensely poised on the edge of a chair by the bedside, as though he was about ready to be off somewhere. He was naked to the waist, the muscles of his chest and arms rippling as he braced his good hand against the seat. His skin was lightly bronzed and for the most part undamaged, at least from the oblique angle which was her main line of vision. He was, though, as far as Jassie could make out from his expression, thoroughly irritable.

A pretty, dark-haired nurse was there alongside him, trying unsuccessfully to persuade him to put on a pair of pyjamas and get into bed. She was very young, and appeared to be totally fazed by the level of opposition she was getting. Alex's expression looked every bit like that of a mutinous young boy.

'For the last time,' he said, scowling, 'I am not staying here. I want my shirt, and I want to leave, now.'

'But you're not in any condition to leave,' the girl protested. 'Think about it...you've had quite extensive second-degree burns, and your lungs might have been damaged by smoke. We need to keep you under observation, at least for a while.'

'I'm not going to argue with you,' he said with a rasp, then started to cough. He recovered, wincing, having trouble with his breathing, then added, 'I meant what I said. I'm getting out of here. I have things to do.'

'Such as?' Jassie shut the door behind her and walked into the room.

Alex twisted around, his brows shooting up. 'Jassie—what are you doing here?'

She had a good chance now to see the extent of his injuries, and she had to bite her lip to stop herself from showing her distress.

'I'm rescuing this poor girl from your bad temper, as far as I can see. Why are you giving her such a hard time? She's only trying to help you.'

'If she wants to help me, she can find my shirt for me so that I can get out of here.' He started to cough all over again.

Jassie glanced at the nurse. 'Would you mind giving us a minute?'

'Not at all.' She gave Jassie a rueful smile. 'I won't be too far away if you need me.'

She left the room, and Alex rolled his eyes in relief. 'Thank heaven for that. I thought I might strangle her if she stayed here any longer.'

'You'd have a job, one-handed,' Jassie pointed out with a wry smile. 'Look at you. Your hand's wrapped up in a plastic bag and, in case you've forgotten, there are dressings on your shoulder and back.'

The dressings were of a type used specifically for burns. They were designed to keep the area moist in order to promote healing, and the burns would possibly have been treated with an antibacterial agent.

She said drily, 'I shouldn't think you're in any condition to strangle as much as a flea. How did you manage to get yourself into such a state? I heard you'd been flown here in a helicopter. I was really worried about you.'

He frowned. 'Were you?'

'Yes, I was,' she said seriously. 'I think I almost expected to find you lying here, semi-conscious.'

He smiled at her. 'I'm OK, as you can see.'

'I'd say that's a debatable point.' She grimaced, her gaze moving over the large expanse of his back that was covered by a dressing. It took up a good quarter. 'So, tell me what happened?'

'The lifeboat crew received an SOS message and I had to go out to help with some of the injured men. A gas bottle had exploded on board ship, and one of the crew was trapped in the hold. He'd broken his leg, and he was screaming at us to get him out of there.' He paused for a moment, his breath coming in ragged spurts. Watching him, Jassie started to feel anxious all over again.

'Well, you can imagine,' he went on. 'He was terrified that we would go away and leave him but, of course, we didn't. The fire crew were a tremendous bunch. They moved heaven and earth to get to him.'

He stopped for a moment to allow his lungs time to recover. 'Anyway, eventually between us we managed to free him, and then I went with him in the helicopter to make sure he was OK. His circulation was compromised and I wanted to make sure that he wouldn't lose the leg.'

'Is he going to be all right?'

'I think so. Last I heard they were operating on him, and the surgeon thought his chances were good.'

'And you? How are you, really? You don't look so good, from what I can see.'

'It doesn't feel as bad as you might expect. In fact, when it first happened, it didn't register properly.' He gave her a rueful smile. 'It was only when I was in the helicopter that it started to hurt like hell, but they gave me a painkilling injection when I was brought in here. I was glad of that, I can tell you.'

'I can imagine you were. Has the doctor talked to you about the degree of the burns and how they might heal?'

He nodded. 'It looks as though I might get away without any scarring. I'm lucky, I guess.'

'You're very lucky, if that's the case. I could hardly believe it when I heard the reports on the local news.' She pulled a face and said pointedly, 'It seems to me that I can't leave you alone for five minutes without you getting yourself into trouble.' She paused, looking thoughtful for a moment. 'Now, where have I heard that one before?'

He grinned. 'I can see you're on good form today. Sassy, aren't you? Look, why don't you help me to get out of here? Then maybe we can talk properly.' He sent her an appealing look from under dark lashes, his mouth curved in boyish persuasion. 'That nurse is going to be back any minute, threatening me with sedation and the like, and I shall only finish up by upsetting her.'

'No, you won't. I shan't let you do that. She's barely more than a child and you ought to be ashamed of yourself for giving her a bad time. It's in your own interest to stay in hospital and have your condition monitored. Why are you being so unreasonable? It isn't like you—you're normally such a considerate man.'

He managed to look shamefaced. 'I didn't mean to

take it out on her. It's just that I hate the thought of being stuck in hospital. I know I'll be no good as a patient. I don't want people fussing round me, taking my temperature every five minutes and doing all manner of investigations.'

Jassie laughed. 'Alex, how can you say that? You're a doctor. You send people to hospital all the time.'

'It isn't funny,' he said in an aggrieved tone. 'I'm being deadly serious. I thought I might at least be able to depend on you to help me out.'

Still laughing, Jassie walked to the door. 'I'll see what I can do,' she said, 'but just remember this—if I get you out of here, you owe me one.'

He made a growling response, which she didn't quite catch because she was already off in search of the nurse.

'Is that Dr Beaufort's shirt?' she asked, finding her at the nursing station bundling a few assorted belongings into a carrier bag.

'There's not much left of it,' the girl said, viewing the scorched remnant dubiously. 'I don't think he'll really want it back, do you?'

Jassie shook her head. 'No, I shouldn't think so. You can let him have his other things, though—his wallet and his watch, and whatever else there is that's still in decent condition. He's determined that he's going to leave here, and I really don't think there's any way of getting him to change his mind. He's not going to listen to reason, so I'll take him home with me and I'll accept responsibility for taking care of him.'

The nurse gave a wry smile. 'You'll have your hands full. Anyway, his belongings are all here. Tell him he needs to sign for them on his way out and I'll have his medication waiting for him here as well.'

'I'll do that. Thanks.'

A few minutes later, she shepherded Alex towards her car. He was still coughing, and the air outside made him struggle a little with his breathing.

'Are you sure you're up to this?' she asked him with a frown as she helped him into the passenger seat. 'Are you in pain? Do your lungs feel sore?'

'They're not too bad. The registrar gave me something to make my lungs feel easier.'

'You could still suffer from other after-effects, you know. Delayed shock, for instance.'

'I'll be fine.'

'Hmm. We'll see. I'll take you home and keep you company for tonight, just to make sure. That's the price you have to pay for me bailing you out.'

Given his grouchy behaviour on the ward, she half expected him to object, but to her surprise he accepted her ultimatum easily enough.

'I thought you would still be with Rob.'

'He seems to be a lot better, and I decided he could manage without me for a while. Besides, his family is with him now. I think they're planning on taking him back to London with them.'

'Are they? And what about you?' He frowned. 'Will you be going with him?'

'How can I do that? I have a job here, remember? And since you're going to be out of action for a while, you'll need me to hang around, won't you?'

'Hmm. I don't know about that. I can manage by myself. I'm not a child.'

'Stop arguing with me, Alex,' she said firmly. 'I'm here, and you're not getting rid of me that easily.'

Once they had arrived at his house, she set about making him feel more comfortable, settling him on the sofa and making sure that he had adequate fluids to drink. Although she had kept up a light-hearted banter with him, she was actually quite concerned that when the tablets wore off he would be in considerable pain, and the possibility of shock was a real one. She wanted to be close at hand, just in case.

As it was, the horrors of the day gradually caught up with him, and he eventually told her more about what had happened, and how they had worked with the injured people on board.

'It's not something I'd want to go through again in a hurry,' he said in a quiet voice. 'But it could have been worse. At least there were no fatalities.'

She listened and sympathised, but as the evening wore on she could see that it was all beginning to catch up with him.

'Why don't you let me help you get to bed?' she murmured softly.

He laughed huskily, then battled for breath as his lungs rebelled. 'Now, there's an invitation I've waited to hear for a long time... Too bad I'm not in a fit state to do anything about it.'

'Isn't it just?' Her blue eyes flashed a scornful acknowledgement. 'So, come on, then, lean on me and I'll help you upstairs. You look as though you're wiped out.'

He wasn't arguing with her, and between them they managed to slowly negotiate the stairs. Jassie took him to his room and helped him lie down on the bed on his uninjured side. She wasn't going to attempt to help him to undress, not after the comments he had made downstairs, but she removed his shoes and socks and then gently covered him with a blanket.

'I'll be in the room next door if you need me,' she murmured soothingly. 'Try to get some rest.'

She went and lay down on the bed in the guest room, next to his. For a while she stared into space, thinking over the events of the last few hours and wondering at how much things could change in just a very short time, but after a while her eyes closed and she must at last have fallen asleep.

Something woke her. Startled, she sat up and for a moment she wondered where she was, feeling thoroughly disorientated and confused. It was very dark, and she realised that it must be the early hours of the morning. Then she heard the sound of breaking glass from the room next door and after that a muttered curse, and all the events of the day came flooding back.

Rushing into Alex's room, she saw that he was struggling with a bottle of tablets, and that the glass of water she had left on his bedside table was now a puddle of shattered fragments on the floor.

'Wretched thing slipped out of my hand,' he muttered. 'Sorry. I didn't mean to wake you. I was trying to take some painkillers.'

'You should have called me. That's why I'm here. There's no need for you to struggle on your own. I could have helped you with your tablets.'

'I didn't want to disturb you.'

'Well, I'm here now. I'll fetch another glass, and then I'll clear up. Don't you try to touch anything.'

Obediently for a change, he did as he was told, and when she had finally managed to settle him back against his pillows once more, he reached out with his good arm and tugged her down beside him.

'Thanks for being here, Jassie. You're an angel.'

'Of course I am. You don't know how lucky you are,' she returned impishly.

He curved his arm around her, bringing her closer to him, so that she was snuggled into the warmth of his chest, her legs tangling with the solid musculature of his thighs. She hadn't been this close to him for what seemed like an age, and the delicious intimacy and the desire to be held firmly in his arms once more were too compelling to resist.

'Mmm...that feels nice,' he murmured drowsily, and she guessed that the tablets were beginning to take effect. She didn't want to move away and risk disturbing him, and after a while she felt his cheek resting lightly against her hair, heard the gentle sound of his breathing and realised that he was asleep once more.

She was more than happy to stay where she was, but perhaps that wasn't altogether a good idea. In the morning, it could bring about all sorts of complications. He had been in pain, and perhaps hadn't been thinking too clearly. He might be embarrassed to remember how he had pulled her down beside him, and she didn't want to see the dismay at his impulsive action register in his eyes in the cool light of day. She really ought to leave him now and go back to her room.

When she tried to gently extricate herself, though, he gave a ragged sigh and his arm tightened around her, pulling her even further into the curve of his body.

Oh, well. Maybe it would be simpler just to give in and stay where she was. And anyway, if she was honest with herself, it was really the only place she wanted to be.

Contented, Jassie closed her eyes and fell soundly asleep, not waking until the sunlight danced on her eyelids in the morning and teased her into wakefulness.

Alex was still sleeping beside her, peacefully now, his face relaxed, a faint smile hovering around his mouth and testifying to pleasant dreams. Jassie looked down at him and couldn't resist the urge to place a gentle kiss on his mouth, one so tender and fleeting that he barely stirred.

Careful not to disturb him, she eased herself off the bed and went into the bathroom.

A few minutes later, she went downstairs to the kitchen and made a start on preparing breakfast.

Alex appeared after some twenty minutes or so, sniffing the air. 'That smells good.'

'Bacon and eggs,' she told him, glancing up and seeing that he had changed into a clean shirt and trousers. 'You seem to have managed to wash and dress yourself all right. I wondered how you would cope.'

'It wasn't too difficult, just slow, that's all.' He rubbed his jawline with the fingers of his uninjured hand. 'I had a shave, too, so I'm less of a grizzly bear this morning. Thank heaven for electric shavers.'

'Are you feeling a bit better this morning?'

'Much better, thanks.'

She smiled. 'It's amazing what a good night's sleep can do.'

'Isn't it?' His tawny eyes flickered brilliantly. 'You must have slept soundly.'

A flush of heat spread along her cheekbones as she remembered the way she had fallen asleep in his embrace. Still, at least he couldn't have any idea that she had spent last night curled up in his arms, could he?

'Perhaps I'm more relaxed now that Rob is well again and I can concentrate on other things.'

'I gathered that. You slept like a baby, cosy in my bed, safe and secure.'

Jassie's eyes widened and her mouth went suddenly dry. Surely he was guessing? He had been asleep the whole time, hadn't he?

'How...?' Her voice cracked and she started again. 'How would you know anything about how and where I slept? You were well away in dreamland once you had swallowed your tablets.'

'Not for the whole of the night,' he murmured softly. 'I seem to remember waking up once or twice.'

'Did you?' She winced inwardly, then tried a nonchalant shrug. 'I wouldn't know anything about that. I only know that you seemed to need my company to help you to get some rest. Burns can be nasty, can't they? Quite indescribably painful, and not easily soothed.'

Alex lifted a dark brow. 'Are you trying to change the subject? Why does it bother you that you slept with me?'

'I didn't sleep with you—not in any sense that

you're implying,' she retorted crossly, turning back to the hob so that he wouldn't see the heat that suddenly flushed her cheeks. She slapped eggs and bacon onto warmed plates. 'I don't know why you're trying to make something of it. I'd have thought that you would want to forget that it ever happened.'

He looked startled. 'Why would I want to do that? I'd much rather it happened more often...especially if I was fully fit and I wasn't hampered by these wretched burns.' He sent her a wickedly mischievous smile.

'Is that what you really think? Only a couple of weeks back you were implying that I would soon be rushing off back to London. How come you've changed your mind all of a sudden? Do you think maybe you can persuade me into having a casual fling with you and then, when you've had enough of me, you can send me on my way again? If that's what's going on in your head, I'll tell you here and now that you can forget that idea.' She glared at him, sliding his plate forcefully across the table.

He stopped it with one hand before it could disappear over the edge. His eyes narrowed. 'Have I hit a nerve here? Why am I suddenly getting so much flak? I don't remember saying that I wanted you out of the way.'

'No? So what was all that about nothing being set in stone, and maybe I'd be better off going back to London?'

'I thought that was where you wanted to be. You only ever came here because you were feeling low after breaking up with Rob, and you wanted a fresh start. Now that he's taken the trouble to come down here to find you, I guessed you would want to go back home with him.'

'Funny, that,' she said tartly, slamming the grill door shut. 'I was beginning to think I was home already...here.'

His eyes widened. 'Is that what you really think? That this is your home?'

'Why shouldn't I?' She faced him across the table, her hands gripping the back of a chair.

'Aren't you planning to go back to London with Rob?'

'I don't have any plans to be with Rob. He means a lot to me, because we were close once and we were going to be married, but I know that we would never have been happy together. It would have been a mistake to go through with it.' She frowned. 'We'll always be friends, though. Is that so hard for you to understand?'

Alex shook his head, looking fazed by what Jassie had said. 'Not hard...but I didn't think I would ever hear you say it with such conviction. I've waited a long time for you to be sure of yourself, to know for certain what it is you want.'

'Haven't I always said that I wanted to stay here?'

'That's true. I wanted to believe it, I wanted you to stay here with me, but there was so much else going on in your life that I couldn't convince myself that you knew your own mind.'

She swallowed. 'Do you really mean that?' she asked huskily. 'That you want me to be here with you?'

He looked at her steadily, his eyes warm and golden. 'I mean it.'

Bemused, she said unevenly, 'But you seemed so sure that I would go away, and it almost seemed to me that you wouldn't much care if I did. Sometimes it felt as though you were pushing me away. You even drew up a short-list of doctors to take my place.'

He looked puzzled. 'Short-list?'

'Dr Ellis...wasn't he on the list to fill the vacancy? There's no point denying it—I know you were looking at suitable candidates.'

'To take John's place. He's due to retire very soon, and I'll need to get someone in to fill his shoes. We're a four-doctor practice, remember?'

She was dumbfounded. Recovering after a moment or two, she said huskily, 'So you weren't trying to push me away?'

'I wasn't. But I had to be sure that you knew what you really wanted. I didn't want you to go...but I felt that it was a decision you had to make on your own, without me influencing you in any way. If I had put pressure on you to stay, I would never have known whether you would have doubts some time in the future, whether you would be hankering for what might have been.'

He grimaced. 'You had such a strong relationship with Rob, and I saw how much you cared for him when he was ill, that I was suddenly afraid you would rediscover your feelings for him. I was desperate to have you turn to me, but how could I persuade you that I was the one man who could make you happy, knowing that he was always going to be there in the background? I needed you to work through this, and be absolutely certain that you were doing the right thing.'

Jassie blinked, trying to take in all that he was saying. 'But you didn't say any of this to me. You didn't tell me anything of how you felt.'

'I couldn't, not with Rob on the scene. I do want you, Jassie, I need you to be part of my life, and I hoped that you would understand that. Haven't you known it all along, deep down?'

'I knew that you wanted me,' she began huskily, 'but I...I need more than just an affair, Alex. I've never gone in for simple, live-in relationships. I'm old-fashioned in that way, I suppose.'

He came towards her. 'That's a relief. I'm glad about that, because so am I.' He reached for her, his arm going around her, his hand flattening on the curve of her spine.

'I love you, Jassie. I think I've known that, deep down, ever since the moment you walked into my arms that night at the Harbour Inn. You were so sweet and lovely, and then so shocked because you had made a mistake, that I wanted to bundle you up in my arms and carry you away.'

'But you didn't want me here,' she objected. 'That's why you insisted on the six months' trial period.'

'You seemed so young and somehow vulnerable, and I couldn't be sure that you knew for certain what it was you wanted. Then I found out about Rob, and I had to try to fight the way I felt about you, but it was always a losing battle.' He gave her a wry smile. 'I knew there was so much else going on in your life, and you might only have turned to me on the rebound. I didn't want to risk that. I needed you to be absolutely sure of your feelings.'

'I've known for a long time that I love you,' she said softly, 'but I was afraid to follow my instincts. I made mistakes before, and I didn't want to do the same again. I was scared that if I let myself care for you too much, I would end up getting badly hurt if you didn't feel the same way about me.'

'You don't have to be scared of anything. I'll never hurt you, Jassie. I want you with my heart and my soul, and I can't imagine what my life would be without you. This last week while I've been watching you with Rob have been torture for me.'

He lowered his head and found her mouth, kissing her tenderly, and it felt so natural, so perfect that suddenly she knew that everything was going to be all right from this moment on.

'I was so desperately worried when I heard that you had gone out with the lifeboat,' she confided against his cheek. 'I didn't know what I would do if anything had happened to you.'

'I'm safe, I'm here with you, and that's how I want it to be from now on,' he said, gently brushing a stray tendril of hair from her cheek and tucking it behind her ear. 'I want you with me all the time, for us to live together as man and wife. Say that you'll marry me, Jassie? Put me out of my misery.'

'I will,' she murmured softly, reaching up to kiss him again, and when his lips met hers, she knew that she had truly come home, once and for all.

After a while, when they came up for air, he murmured, 'We'll have to let Eva Marriott know what you plan to do about the cottage.'

'The cottage?' She was pensive for a moment. 'I'll be sorry to leave it. It's so beautiful up there.'

'You don't have to leave it. We'll put in an offer to buy it, if that's what you want. I'm sure Eva will accept.'

'That would be wonderful.' Jassie sighed happily, kissing him firmly on the mouth. 'You've made all my dreams come true.'

'Not quite all of them,' he murmured, laughing softly. 'There could be more to come.' His mouth gently teased her lips, and she kissed him again, loving the feel of him, the way their bodies meshed in perfect unison.

It was a long time before they surfaced from that loving embrace, and an even longer time before either of them noticed that the breakfast she had cooked was now well and truly cold.

'Oh, well,' Alex said, 'not to worry. We could always have toast and coffee instead.' Then with a teasing smile, he added, 'Breakfast in bed would be good, don't you think?'

'Sounds wonderful,' she murmured. 'Are you sure you're up to it?'

'Try me,' he said with a laugh, and kissed her all over again.

Modern Romance™
...seduction and
passion guaranteed

Tender Romance™
...love affairs that
last a lifetime

Sensual Romance™
...sassy, sexy and
seductive

Blaze
...sultry days and
steamy nights

Medical Romance™
...medical drama on
the pulse

Historical Romance™
...rich, vivid and
passionate

29 new titles every month.

*With all kinds of Romance for
every kind of mood...*

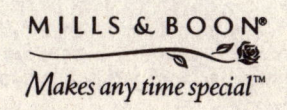

MILLS & BOON®
Makes any time special™

MAT4

MILLS & BOON

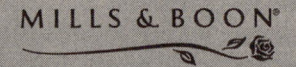

Medical Romance™

A WOMAN WORTH WAITING FOR
by Meredith Webber

Dr Detective – Down Under

After five years Ginny is still the beautiful, caring woman Max remembers, and a wonderful emergency nurse. But she clearly hasn't forgiven him. It takes a murder investigation to bring them together, and in their new-found closeness, Max knows that he'd wait for this woman for ever...

A NURSE'S COURAGE by Jessica Matthews

Part 3 of Nurses Who Dare

ER nurse Rachel Wyman has come back to Hooper to think about a new career. But Nick Sheridan adores Rachel, he needs her – and so does Hooper General Hospital. He's determined to help Rachel conquer her fears about nursing, and win her love, but does she have the courage to take them both on?

THE GREEK SURGEON by Margaret Barker

Sister Demelza Tregarron found herself hoping against hope that Dr Nick Capodistrias and his young son could be the family she'd longed for. In Nick's arms the life she had dreamed about seemed within reach. But when his ex-wife reappeared, Demelza feared she was about to lose those she loved...all over again.

On sale 5th April 2002

Available at most branches of WH Smith, Tesco, Martins, Borders, Eason, Sainsbury's and most good paperback bookshops.

MILLS & BOON®

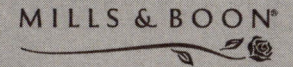

Medical Romance™

DOCTOR IN NEED by *Margaret O'Neill*

Nurse Fiona McFie was damned if she was going to let Tom Cameron walk all over her – and the uneasy attraction that simmered between them made her want to fight him even more. But Tom proved to be a talented doctor and a devoted father, and soon Fiona realised that all she really wanted was to give Tom and his children all the love they could ever need!

TEMPTING DR TEMPLETON by *Judy Campbell*

A 'bonding' course certainly isn't Dr Rosie Loveday's idea of fun – until she meets her gorgeous instructor, Dr Andy Templeton. Their mutual sparks of attraction are impossible to ignore, but Rosie is determined to stay single. It's up to Andy to persuade her otherwise and he's got the *perfect* plan!

MOTHER ON CALL by *Jean Evans*

Even though it meant juggling single motherhood with a new job, Beth moved to Cornwall so that she could start being a GP again. Then an embarrassing encounter with Sam Armstrong, the new senior partner, marked the beginning of a tense working relationship, made worse by the chemistry they shared. Sooner or later something – or someone – would have to give...

On sale 5th April 2002

Available at most branches of WH Smith, Tesco, Martins, Borders, Eason, Sainsbury's and most good paperback bookshops.

Treat yourself this Mother's Day to the ultimate indulgence

3 brand new romance novels and a box of chocolates

= *only £7.99*

Available from 15th February

Available at most branches of WH Smith, Tesco, Martins, Borders, Eason, Sainsbury's and most good paperback bookshops.

0202/91/MB32

MIRANDA LEE
Secrets & Sins revealed

SEDUCED BY HER BODYGUARD AND STALKED BY A STRANGER...

Available from 15th March 2002

*Available at most branches of WH Smith,
Tesco, Martins, Borders, Eason, Sainsbury's
and most good paperback bookshops.*

FREE

2 BOOKS
AND A SURPRISE GIFT!

We would like to take this opportunity to thank you for reading this Mills & Boon® book by offering you the chance to take **TWO** more specially selected titles from the Medical Romance™ series absolutely **FREE**! We're also making this offer to introduce you to the benefits of the Reader Service™—

- ★ FREE home delivery
- ★ FREE monthly Newsletter
- ★ FREE gifts and competitions
- ★ Exclusive Reader Service discount
- ★ Books available before they're in the shops

Accepting these FREE books and gift places you under no obligation to buy; you may cancel at any time, even after receiving your free shipment. Simply complete your details below and return the entire page to the address below. ***You don't even need a stamp!***

YES! Please send me 2 free Medical Romance books and a surprise gift. I understand that unless you hear from me, I will receive 4 superb new titles every month for just £2.55 each, postage and packing free. I am under no obligation to purchase any books and may cancel my subscription at any time. The free books and gift will be mine to keep in any case.

M2ZEC

Ms/Mrs/Miss/Mr .... Initials ....
BLOCK CAPITALS PLEASE

Surname ....

Address ....

....

.... Postcode ....

Send this whole page to:
UK: FREEPOST CN81, Croydon, CR9 3WZ
EIRE: PO Box 4546, Kilcock, County Kildare (stamp required)

Offer valid in UK and Eire only and not available to current Reader Service subscribers to this series. We reserve the right to refuse an application and applicants must be aged 18 years or over. Only one application per household. Terms and prices subject to change without notice. Offer expires 30th June 2002. As a result of this application, you may receive offers from other carefully selected companies. If you would prefer not to share in this opportunity please write to The Data Manager at the address above.

Mills & Boon® is a registered trademark owned by Harlequin Mills & Boon Limited.
Medical Romance™ is being used as a trademark.